THE FINAL
DESTINATION

THE FINAL
DESTINATION

SISTER DIANE CAROLLO, S.G.L.

The Final Destination

ISBN: 978-1-941142-02-8

Printed in the United States

Acknowledgements

My thanks to the O'Brien family and Mary Ann Garber for their constructive criticisms and help in the final editing of this book.

Author's Note

"Truth must necessarily be stranger than fiction; for fiction is the creation of the human mind and therefore congenial to it."

—*G.K. Chesterton*

The Final Destination is a work of fiction—a fantasy that is meant to invite the reader to consider what traditional Catholic theology distinguishes as the Four Last Things—death, judgment, Heaven (most likely after the experience of Purgatory) and Hell. The events related may seem bizarre because they describe something that is far beyond the understanding of the living. However, because the human mind is finite and cannot begin to grasp or imagine what the afterlife will actually be like, we can assume that the reality will be even more beyond our understanding.

The experience of the antechamber of Hell described in the novel is not an article of Catholic faith. It is an imaginary place that brings the characters in the story to understand fully the horror of sin and its consequences.

The truth is that every person will appear before the judgment seat of Christ immediately after death when the soul separates from the body (cf. 2 Corinthians 5:10, Hebrews 4:13 and 1 Peter 4:5). However, no one can be sure what happens in the critical split second *before* the soul leaves the body. This novel is an imaginative look at what *might* occur while a soul hovers momentarily on the brink of death…

The possibility of the eternal loss of Heaven should alarm any rational person, and the prospect of such a dreadful fate should motivate all human beings to take a daily inventory of their spiritual lives. With informed consciences, we should examine the manner in which we live our daily lives and resolve to do the will of God in all things.

My ultimate desire is that *The Final Destination* will inspire readers to make life-giving choices that lead to the kingdom where Love reigns eternally.

Laura O'Malley has been chosen to describe her experiences and those of several others as they crossed the boundary from life to death, from time to eternity, on a day that started much like any other day...

1

LAURA O'MALLEY

7:10 A.M. Jan 18th
Brooklyn N.Y.

A S THE TRAIN pulled out of the subway station, I thought ahead to my job interview with Dr. David Steinfeld, M.D., my prospective employer. I had applied for a position as a physician's assistant at Innovative Health Care Options, a medical center in Lower Manhattan. Although many conservative groups had criticized the center for its experimentation on human embryos, IHCO had been an astounding financial success. I was currently employed as a physician's assistant at a small local hospital. Working under Dr. Steinfeld would definitely be a step up for my career.

Eventually my thoughts wandered to my fellow passengers who had also braved the snow-covered streets of Brooklyn to reach the station. There were several people on the train, but only a few caught my attention. I particularly noticed a dark, nervous-looking bearded man muttering something under his breath; a young African-American dividing his attention between the crossword puzzle on his lap and a photograph in his hand; a woman of about 30 who seemed to be near tears; and a pony-tailed man in his thirties who was holding a manuscript. I couldn't help but notice the title of the manuscript: *The Myth of Christianity*. As a Catholic (though admittedly only a nominal one), I was mildly intrigued.

As I pulled out my iPod to listen to my favorite Josh Groban album, I glanced at the time: 7:20. The train was right on time, and should pull into Manhattan about 20 minutes before my scheduled appointment. I leaned back in my seat and closed my eyes, only to open them again seconds later to the sound of screams. The man with the beard was standing up and shouting something unintelligible, but I clearly understood his intention as he gestured wildly with a small device in his hand. During the split-second before the explosion, all that had time to flash through my mind was a horrible fear of dying and an intense hatred for the bearded man.

2

LAURA O'MALLEY

THE NEXT THING I knew, I was lying on my face with pieces of the train landing all around me. The only light was a bright reddish-orange glow coming from the gaping hole in the portion of the train where the bomber had been seated. Everyone else was mangled horribly; with the corner of my mind that wasn't too dazed to think, I was shocked to find that I wasn't dead and didn't even seem hurt. Apparently, I was the only survivor.

I reached for my cell phone to call the police and report the blast, only to realize that I must have left it on the dresser in my apartment. Standing up, I quickly made my way to the twisted door separating the train compartments and tried to yank it open, but it refused to budge. Looking through the shattered window of the door, I saw that the other train compartment seemed to have vanished. My only escape route had to be from the end of the train where the bomb had been detonated. In spite of a growing feeling of dread, I began to edge toward the strange, fiery light from outside the compartment.

From the exposed end of the train compartment, I jumped onto the tracks, remembering at the last second to avoid the electrified third rail. I decided to walk along the tracks back to the Thirty-Sixth Street station in Brooklyn, figuring that the blast had been reported to the authorities, and that all trains would be rerouted or held.

What still puzzled me was that following the detonation of the bomb I had felt no pain and was virtually unaffected by the blast. To be the only survivor and not even sustain any injuries didn't make sense. I turned to look back at the wreckage and was shocked to see that the train compartment was engulfed in a cloud of darkness. Focusing only on getting to safety, I decided not even to try to understand my experience.

As I walked toward what I thought was safety, I noticed a male figure in the distance coming toward me. Could that be someone coming to help? I wondered about the rescue crews and how long it might take the authorities to mobilize them.

As the man approached, I halted and cried out, "Please, help me. There was an explosion on the train. I think everyone else is dead!"

The stranger said nothing for a moment, but only smiled. Then he said smoothly, "Yes, that was quite an explosion, Laura! Magnificent, wasn't it?" He held out his arms as if to embrace me.

"What? Magnificent? Some maniac just killed everyone in my compartment!" I paused, then demanded, "How do you know my name?"

Ignoring my question, and still smiling, the man responded, "That explosion was a work of art. It was ingenious!"

I froze where I was standing. "What do you mean? Are you crazy? Where are the police and the rescue crews?"

The man looked ordinary enough – handsome and in his early thirties – but I began to suspect that he might be the terrorist's accomplice. I backed away from him.

"Stop!" he ordered. "You will do as I say."

I found myself unable to move an inch. The man's smile vanished, and his bright blue eyes suddenly became lifeless and cold. He stood a couple of feet away from me and extended his hand. I watched in confusion and horror as my hand was raised to his icy lips by some unseen force, despite my attempt to resist.

The stranger made one final comment before I was compelled to follow him. "I'm not crazy at all, Laura. I've been waiting for you. You'll find out all about me soon enough."

Meanwhile, although the other passengers appeared dead to me, each of them was undergoing a similar experience. Yet they all had a unique story to tell…

3

CATHY PETERSEN

CATHY PETERSEN MOANED as she rolled onto her side and propped herself up on her elbow. The large handbag she had carried had fallen to the ground. She frantically rummaged through its contents, now littered on the floor. Relieved, Cathy reached for an envelope; it contained the important receipt that had been the reason for her trip to Manhattan that morning.

Looking up, Cathy was sickened by the sight of dead bodies scattered around the train compartment. Rising to her feet, she frantically searched for a quick exit. As her eyes focused on the gaping hole at the opposite end of the compartment, she could see the subway tracks below. A reddish-orange light from the tunnel illuminated her immediate surroundings. It took all the courage she could muster to step over my mutilated lifeless body and the barely recognizable remains of the other travelers.

She glanced back only once; concluding that she was the sole survivor of the explosion, she stumbled down the tracks toward the previous train station. When she reached for her cell phone, she cursed under her breath at the discovery that there was no service. Frustrated, she continued until she saw a figure in the distance. The eerie light that illuminated the tracks revealed the approach of a handsome young man with dark hair.

"Help!" Cathy shouted. "A suicide bomber…on my train…I think they're all dead!" Even as she was speaking, she distinctly heard the man whisper her name several times. He reached to embrace her, but she stepped back, bewildered. "Wait a minute! Who are you? How do you know my name?"

Although attractive, the stranger was beginning to seem slightly sinister, especially when he made his reply, "I've known you for quite a long time, Cathy."

Shaking her head in disbelief, Cathy insisted, "No. I've never met you before." She felt even more threatened as he ignored her words and condescendingly offered his arm to lead her. "Who are you?" she demanded, with fear in her voice.

The stranger smiled, "I was sent here to help you. You believe in angels, don't you?" Cathy nodded her head. "Well then, I'm your angel. Follow me!"

"You're my guardian angel?"

The stranger only laughed.

4

DA'RELL THOMAS

THE CROSSWORD PUZZLE that Da'rell Thomas had been working on was his last memory before the explosion. Sprawled on the floor, he slowly opened his eyes, and with some hesitation, sat up. Carefully rising to his feet, he walked around the compartment. Clearly, there were no other survivors. He was grateful to be unhurt. He recalled the advice his Grandmother, Pearl Thomas, had repeated so many times, "Da'rell, don't always trust what you see. Trust what you know to be true."

He shook his head and said aloud, "I trust that I'm alive, and that's enough for now, Grandma Pearl!"

He noticed the same reddish-orange light that Cathy and I were seeing. At first it provided a sense of security; he had never overcome his childish fear of total darkness. However, the longer he was exposed to the glow, the less secure he felt; it began to seem almost threatening. By its light he made his way to the end of the car and onto the tracks toward safety, hoping to encounter other survivors along the way. He quickened his pace as he headed back to the Thirty-Sixth Street station.

Not more than a few hundred yards beyond the train, he felt someone watching him. He turned to the wreckage behind him; there stood a man who motioned for him to come back, yelling, "Da'rell, wait a minute. I can help you."

Da'rell studied the man, who appeared unhurt from the explosion. "Who are you? Were you on the train, too?"

"Yeah, I was there," the man nodded.

"How do you know my name?"

"I knew everyone on the train! Sorry, I don't mean to be rude; my name is Eric Luf. Follow me." Da'rell, wary of the man's overly familiar manner, hesitated and started to shake his head. The stranger watched as Da'rell refused to move. Changing his friendly demeanor, he ordered, "Don't dally, boy. Follow me."

"I'm not your boy!" Da'rell shot back defensively.

The tall man ran his hand over his dark hair, preening himself. He sneered, "You are who I say you are! You'll do what I say to do!"

"C'mon man, who are you?"

The stranger snapped, "I'm the one who calls the shots! Now no more questions; move. I won't tell you again."

Da'rell suddenly felt bound by an invisible rope tugging at his waist. Attempts to resist the rope and the stranger's command were futile; tension from the invisible rope yanked him facedown onto the tracks.

"Now, boy, you don't want me to get rough with you, do you? Get on your feet and do as I say!"

Da'rell stood up and followed Eric Luf. With each step, he became more fearful and anxious. He suppressed his impulse to yell at the stranger as he realized that he was physically, if not mentally, under the mysterious man's control. He wondered if the man had any power over his soul.

The stranger walked briskly, but paused for a few seconds; he seemed to read Da'rell's thoughts. In a voice that echoed through the tunnel, he cried out, "I am the one who exercises complete dominion over human life!"

5

JAMES SIMONELLI, PH.D.

JAMES REMOVED THE debris covering his body. Only seconds before, he had heard the bomber shout some foreign words before the bright flash lit up the train. Now the windows were shattered and darkness encompassed the train. The only illumination came from the eerie reddish-orange light that we were also seeing.

James gaped in shock at the gruesome collection of dead bodies around the train compartment. After somewhat regaining his composure, he moved toward the end of the compartment where the light was strongest. He, too, determined that his best route of escape had to be through the tunnel and back to the Thirty-Sixth Street station in Brooklyn.

James hastened through the tunnel, wondering why only he had been spared from the effects of the blast. He was startled, but also relieved, to see a man walking toward him from the direction of the station. The stranger greeted him warmly, "James, James, I'm so glad to see you." As James paused and stared at the man, he continued, "Hi, I'm Eric Luf."

"Eric Luf might be your name. But who *are* you? What are you doing here? And how do you know my name?"

"Well, James, aren't you the inquisitive one? Let me not disappoint you. I know how your mind works; you'll appreciate this little puzzle. Rearrange the letters of my name and you will discover my identity."

James formed a mental picture of the letters from the name Eric Luf. Moving the letters out of sequence, he quickly rearranged them to spell out L U C I F E R.

Almost immediately he heard Lucifer cry out, "Good boy! And, yes, Professor Simonelli, I can read your thoughts. Welcome to the antechamber of Hell!"

6

LAURA O'MALLEY

THE STRANGER LAUGHED, apparently amused by my confusion. "Laura, haven't you figured all this out yet? You're an intelligent woman. Use that keen mind of yours to figure out what has happened to you." Afraid to voice my greatest fears, I stood in absolute silence. "My dear, you just died on the train a few minutes ago. No one survived that positively superb explosion. I'm simply here to retrieve my property."

My mind raced. Was I was dazed from the blast and imagining things? This couldn't be happening to me. I wasn't dead! I summoned all my strength and braced myself for one more question. He raised his eyebrows as though he knew what I wanted to ask.

"What do you mean, 'your property'?" I asked, trying to keep my voice steady.

"You belong to me, Laura. *You are* my property. You're dead and you're mine." The fiend crossed his arms and looked at me coldly. As his last words sunk in, he added, "I've been known in many religions by various names and titles. Throughout history, I've been described in many ways, though most people today don't even think I exist. That disbelief works wonderfully to my advantage. Yes, Laura, I am Satan—your master."

I had no doubt that I was face-to-face with the Evil One described in the Bible. "I will never call you master!" I shouted.

"Not only will you lower your voice when you speak to me, but you will use a reverent tone!" Then, with a malicious smile, he added, "You are in the antechamber of Hell. Welcome to *my* world, Laura O'Malley. It's where you belong."

"No!" I gasped. All I wanted to do was to run—but I knew he could easily overtake me. I turned to look back at the train, only to find that it had disappeared into a black void.

"Don't be difficult, Laura. Did you actually think you had a chance for any other fate? Be honest. We both know you turned your back on God long ago! You had no use for the Catholic faith of your parents, or any faith for that matter. I used to love hearing you and your parents argue after you abandoned it. They were concerned for the salvation of your soul, weren't they? I always enjoyed your babbling that you were a 'very spiritual person,' but 'rejected organized religion.' No one had the right to dictate morality to you—not the state, not the Church. Ah, such splendid words to condemn you now! Shall I go on about all the choices you made based on your 'personal morality?' You've earned your reward, my love. You're lost forever!"

I felt deep sorrow and dread at the pronouncement of my sentence. I couldn't argue with him; I had stopped practicing my Catholic faith and had lived an immoral life, especially by my parents' standards. Was I truly reaping what I had sown? I had always told myself that the choices I made were perfectly legitimate.

"Do you know that I can read your thoughts, Laura? I know what you are thinking at this very instant!"

"Then you know that I want no part of you!" I replied.

"There's no need to be rude, and it's already too late for you. You've chosen me consistently for the past six years. It's a done deal, as they say above. Even the most liberal priests admit that a person can choose to go to Hell. They just don't believe anyone would. How wrong they are!"

I closed my eyes, fervently hoping that I had fallen asleep and was having a nightmare, that when I reopened them I would be sitting on the N Train listening to Josh Groban's music. I counted to three and looked up. To my utter surprise, I was no longer in the tunnel, but was standing in what appeared to be a morgue. The creature stood only a few feet away. Metallic drawers lined the walls, while the rest of the room was equipped with tables and tools used for autopsies.

"Laura, welcome to my kingdom," Satan said proudly. "Like you, I'm a 'very spiritual' being. My angelic nature, of course, is far superior to yours! I'm sure you'll be impressed with my powers for all eternity." Boastfully he continued, "I am superior to all the angels. I told my enemy that I would never serve anybody – not God, not man, not the Son of Man, not any of his worthless followers!"

The beast pointed at the wall, and a drawer immediately opened. It was empty.

"Make yourself comfortable inside, Laura. You are a cadaver now!"

Terror filled me as I was lifted by an invisible force. I floated horizontally, suspended above the empty drawer. Although my limbs were paralyzed, my voice was not. I screamed over and over again, hoping I could wake myself up.

Once my body was released, I fell into the drawer with a bone-jarring thump. My skull slammed against the metal with a sickening thud, yet I felt no accompanying pain. I lay immobile as the drawer closed slowly and I found myself entombed in total darkness. All the while, I screamed.

The creature managed to make himself heard over my screaming, as he sneered, "My little pumpkin, here there's no rest for the weary, no peace for the troubled, and no happiness forever. The best is yet to come."

7

Cathy Petersen

ATHY STARED AT the stranger as he laughed at her. "If you're my guardian angel, why are you laughing?"

"I said I am an angel; I didn't say anything about 'guardian,' replied Satan with a smirk on his handsome face. In fact, I'm quite the opposite, what you would call a 'fallen angel.'"

Cathy backed away. "I don't believe in fallen angels," she laughed nervously.

"Oh, you only believe in the angels when they make you feel good? My angels believe in you, Cathy. The fallen ones in my kingdom find you quite attractive, and a wonderful catch, indeed!" Satan said as he moved closer.

"Get away from me!" cried Cathy.

"Is that any way to address someone who has been waiting for you all your life?" taunted Satan.

Cathy held up her hands, shielding herself from his words. "Leave me alone! I don't believe that you're the, the …"

"The Devil?" the creature finished. He looked at Cathy and shook his head disapprovingly. "You do realize you died in the explosion, don't you?"

"No! It can't be true! What do you want from me?"

"It is true, my little dove. You're dead, and you're my trophy."

Cathy stared at Satan with disbelief. "But I was saved! I was saved!"

"Yes, yes, yes! You and millions of others were *'saved.'* But did you really accept salvation? You Christians quibble over things like salvation, and who can be saved, and how. Of course I detest the Catholic Church, but they're right, as much as I hate to acknowledge it; you can't be saved against your will."

He wagged his finger mockingly at his victim. "You certainly didn't want to be saved today!"

"But I'm not Catholic! I was saved once and for all!"

Oh, you Christians! It's so much fun to watch you pitted against each other with your imprecise theological statements. The point is that you *chose* not be saved. That is the bottom line, my little dove." He wagged his finger in Cathy's face again, but this time her focus was drawn to his finger, rather than the gesture. Horrified, she saw that there was now a claw instead of a nail.

Ignoring her reaction, Satan continued, "Don't you see how absurd your claim to be saved is when all you wanted today was to pursue Jason, a married man, and seduce him to sin with you yet again? There's also that decision you made six weeks ago to destroy the child you conceived … Shall I humiliate you by listing all your sins?"

Consumed with guilt, Cathy started to tremble. "This can't be happening to me!"

"Resign yourself to your fate. Abandon all hope. It doesn't exist here."

Cathy screamed as Satan reached out to grab her by the arm. Her voice echoed through the tunnel.

"I love screams! Screams to me are what laughs are to a comedian. There's nothing funny here, though, except the torment of souls."

Cathy sobbed uncontrollably.

"Yes, that's right, cry your heart out. Sadness is what feeds souls down here," Satan informed her pleasantly.

Cathy fought to control her emotions, once she realized how much her antagonist was enjoying her misery.

"Be silent if you wish. You have all eternity to suffer and cry out in agony."

The creature dragged Cathy down the tunnel. He whistled, and she thought she saw four or five children running toward them – but when she looked at them directly, they weren't children at all. They were vicious little demons with pointed teeth, red eyes and long snake-like tongues. They wore filthy, blood-stained garments. Laughing and giggling gleefully, they jumped on her, flung her onto the tracks, and attacked her ferociously.

Cathy tried to defend herself, but she couldn't stop them from scratching and biting her arms and thighs. Satan roared with laughter at her fear and pain, exceeded only by her desperation. Finally Satan gestured for her tormentors to stop. "Leave her alone for now, my little soldiers. You'll have all eternity to play with her. Go now!" The demons, each no more than four feet tall, grunted with disappointment and vanished into thin air.

"Get up, Cathy. Follow me now or I'll call my soldiers back!"

With no will to resist, Cathy rose from the tracks, bloodied and fearful of what lay ahead.

Over and over, she told herself that she had been saved.

"I can read your thoughts, Cathy. Remember that you chose to disobey my enemy's commandments. You chose the path that was forbidden. Honestly, do you think my enemy would *force* you to love, serve and obey him? I can tell you from personal experience that he forces himself on no one. I refused to serve him precisely because I am a superior entity. With one mere thought, no less than a third of the angels joined me in my mission to establish my supremacy. My enemy couldn't force us to serve him or the pathetic humans he created. What makes you think that my enemy would strip you of your free will to serve him? You chose to serve me."

"I never chose to serve you!" she stressed.

"You chose to violate my enemy's laws, and that's as good as choosing me, my little dove," Satan told her with a grin.

8

DA'RELL THOMAS

SATAN WHISTLED AS he led Da'rell, still bound by the invisible rope, along the tracks. Da'rell recognized the tune as "*When the Saints Go Marching In*," and wondered what he had done to deserve this misery. He tried to resist the idea that the man leading him was the devil himself. He shook his head to banish the thought from his mind.

Satan turned to his prisoner. "Your thoughts are quite interesting. Think about the choices you've made in life; they've earned you your reward."

"This is my reward? You're my reward? You've got to be kidding! I'm going to wake up any minute from this nightmare. You're nothing but a figment of my imagination."

"Really! Is that what I am? A figment of your imagination?" Satan stopped and yanked the cord so that Da'rell fell to his knees. "Get up, you lousy pig!" Satan barked. He spoke into the semi-darkness, "Oh, boys, you can come out now, wherever you are! You need to convince my friend how real this is."

The same creatures that had attacked Cathy rushed to his side, licking their lips. Da'rell jumped to his feet and shrieked just as the demons pounced. One bit his arm with razor-sharp teeth; another drew blood on his thigh. Da'rell continued to scream as still another jumped onto his shoulders and clawed at his face, forcing him to the ground. They continued as Satan roared with laughter. "Is this *real* enough for you, boy?"

Finally, as Da'rell begged, "Please! Make them stop!" Satan waved his hand and ordered the demons to leave. "That's enough for now. Be gone." The demons growled, grunted, and reluctantly moved away. With effort Da'rell dragged himself to his feet.

"This is very real, my friend. You're in the antechamber of Hell, and believe me, it only gets better!"

Suddenly Satan shook his head as if he were having a conversation with someone else. "Another guest needs my services," announced the beast. "Use this time to reflect on your past… and your future."

In the blink of an eye, Da'rell found himself standing in a dripping cave barely illuminated by the same glow that he had seen in the tunnel. The hair on the back of his neck stood up as the light began to dim. Beyond the opening of the cave there was only blackness, and the sound of vicious growling nearby, as well as hundreds of voices screaming in torment from a pit opposite the opening.

Exhausted from his encounter with the demons, Da'rell leaned against the wall of the cave and slid down onto the cold dirt floor. He rolled up his sleeves and pant legs to wipe off the blood with his handkerchief. His heart raced as he looked up; the light was almost completely gone. Within seconds, Da'rell could not see his hands as he held them in front of his face. The growling was getting louder; he could hear the demons – sometimes calling his name, sometimes cursing God and His followers, sometimes attacking each other mercilessly. Finally, Da'rell stood up, dreading the demons' next attack and overwhelmed by fear and desperation.

9

JAMES SIMONELLI, PH.D.

A T "ERIC LUF'S" welcome, James put his hands on his hips and laughed. In the most sarcastic tone he could muster, he scoffed, "The antechamber of Hell, indeed! This is absurd!"

Satan pointed to James' wristwatch. "Check the time, professor."

James glanced at his watch. Just before the explosion, it had read 7:20; he saw now that the time had not changed.

"So my watch broke in the blast! What does that prove?"

The creature cleared his throat. "But look at the second hand." It was still moving, though the minute and hour hands had stopped. "Time no longer exists here, professor. That's what happens when you cross the boundary from life to death. Do you really think you walked away from that explosion unscathed?"

James raised his eyebrows.

Satan paced back and forth, pointing his finger at James as he spoke. "I always believed in you—in your ability to destroy what little faith people had. You certainly were an outstanding social scientist! It was brilliant how you converted so many students to your views – to my benefit." Satan started to count on his fingers. "You persuaded at least fifteen students not to believe in my enemy or the afterlife!" Disturbing as the words were, James was distracted from them; his eyes were drawn to Satan's claw-like hand. Satan pulled back his sleeve to show James his own watch. "You'll notice that there aren't any hour and minute hands on my exquisite timepiece. There's only eternity. Here you experience your miserable existence all at once and forever!"

James backed away. "This isn't real. You're not real. There is nothing after death! I don't believe in any of this nonsense!"

Satan laughed. "You're a fool. I'm not an atheist, my dear professor. I am Lucifer, the mighty one, the immortal one, who reigns eternally!"

James shook his head defiantly. "This is a nightmare, nothing more. Period."

"You think this is a nightmare? I didn't mind you denying my existence on Earth, but here you must honor and worship me. I'll show you who you're dealing with, you pathetic creature!" The beast looked menacingly at James. "You're always analyzing things. Maybe you need a more powerful experience of my antechamber to show you what's real. Analyze this!"

Suddenly they were both transported to a small rowboat completely surrounded by water. The starless sky was dark, in spite of a half moon and that unnatural fiery glow around them. James immediately sat down and grabbed the side of the boat with both hands. The beast must have known he had always been afraid of the ocean.

Satan smiled as he stood up and began to rock the boat.

"Stop!" yelled James, forgetting, in his panic, who he was with. "You'll drown us!"

"So, the defiant professor is afraid of the water! More specifically, he's afraid of drowning. Well, you can only die once – on earth, that is. Here you can experience death in oh-so-many delicious ways. You feel the suffering and pangs of death, but… you're already dead! That's what makes it so interesting and entertaining to watch."

Suddenly, James felt water beneath his feet. "Get me out of here!" he screamed, terrified.

"Remember what you said about me?" jeered the creature. "You thought I wasn't real! This is nothing but an illusion; just keep telling yourself that, professor. Enjoy your ride!" He disappeared, leaving behind a foul odor. James choked back vomit as he cowered in the middle of the boat. He reached for the oars, only to find that he was grasping at air – they too had vanished.

It wouldn't take long for the boat to fill up; James' trousers were already saturated with salt water. He removed his shoes and knelt in a futile effort to bail the rapidly rising water. Within minutes, he was drenched and shivering violently from the frigid wind; the muscles in his back and shoulders were already cramping. The sides of the boat sank lower every time he rested even for a moment; he was sure he was only seconds away from drowning. "Help me, Satan!" he cried out. "I believe in you!"

Instantly, the creature reappeared, standing on the water outside the boat. "That's better. Are you ready to do me homage? Take a leap of faith and join me. Take my hand." "I'll do anything you ask. Just get me out of this boat!" James stood up and reached for the claw, but his would-be rescuer sidestepped abruptly, deftly tumbling him into the black ocean.

The professor screamed and flailed his arms, but Satan only laughed maliciously and nodded his head. At that, James found himself and his companion in a deserted arena. Once he composed himself enough to look around, he realized that the arena resembled the Coliseum in Rome.

Again, Satan seemed to read his thoughts. "Yes, my friend, this is a replica of the theatre in Rome, where so many of my enemy's followers died rather than renounce their faith. They were condemned to excruciating death by some of the most illustrious military leaders in human history. I hope you believe in me now, James. I saved you from drowning. Now you must lose your life for me! You have become a believer and I demand that you become my martyr!"

James turned, aghast, toward a number of huge lions pacing in tunnels barred by primitive wooden gates around the arena. "Please, no!" he pleaded. At the sound of his voice, the lions began to roar ferociously.

"Oh yes, James, you must be a martyr for me. You're now a believer. Open the gates, boys!"

Demons appeared and raised the gates, and the lions rushed toward James just as Satan disappeared, laughing heartily. "Let the show begin!" his voice echoed back dramatically.

As the snarling lions encircled James, he did something he had not done since childhood. He prayed. He clasped his hands together and cried out to the Son of God.

"Lord, Jesus, save me!" James repeated his prayer without taking a breath. Suddenly the scene around him changed; the lions and the arena were gone and he found himself bound to a stone pillar.

"You are never to pronounce my enemy's name! You shall be severely punished for your blasphemy," thundered the voice of the still-invisible creature. Unseen whips with metallic barbs lashed at James from every side. He could not see his torturers, but he could hear their laughter each time he cried out in agony. With each stroke, the whips tore more of the skin from his back and legs. Ignoring Satan's warning, as blood and sweat trickled into his eyes and mouth, he cried out to the Lord one last time before losing consciousness.

10

HELEN SIMONELLI-JOHNSON
8:10 a.m.

J UST AS HELEN Simonelli-Johnson started to vacuum the rug in the family room, the telephone rang. She turned off the vacuum and called out to her five-year-old son, "Danny, please answer the phone for Mommy."

Dutifully, Danny ran to the telephone. In a few seconds, he reported, "Daddy wants to talk to you."

Helen wondered what Tom would be calling about; he was so busy running his car dealership that he seldom phoned from work. Hurrying into the kitchen, she picked up the phone. "Is everything all right, Tom?"

Her husband sat at his desk, his eyes glued to the large television screen mounted nearby. On the news, dead and severely wounded passengers were being lifted onto stretchers at the smoke-filled Brooklyn subway station. Tom hesitated, then gulped. "Honey, turn on Fox News."

They listened together to the reporter's words, "New Yorkers are in shock this morning following a terrorist attack in the subway." Gesturing toward the wreckage behind her, she continued, "About an hour ago a bomb was detonated on the N Train between the Thirty-Sixth Street station and the Pacific

Street Station. Here, at Pacific Street, medical personnel are attending some of the wounded. This is the second successful terrorist attack on New York City since 911. Several compartments were severely damaged, but only the compartment where the bomb exploded was completely destroyed. The number of fatalities has not yet been determined. Injured survivors are now being transported to St. Alban's Hospital. Mayor Greenberg is on his way to the scene from Gracie Mansion; he will be issuing a statement shortly."

The mayor appeared on the screen, looking shaken. "Investigators have made a preliminary report;" he announced, "this explosion was most likely the result of a suicide bomber detonating an explosive device. We *will* find and prosecute those who were responsible. Meanwhile, be cautious and vigilant while traveling. Please report anything suspicious immediately to the NYPD."

A reporter called out, "Mayor Greenberg, how can anyone's vigilance protect them from a suicide bomber?"

The mayor ignored the question as he turned away from the cameras and made his way to the street, where medical personnel were loading injured subway riders into ambulances. The camera showed him bending down to comfort a young woman with severe head injuries.

"James called last night while you were picking up Danny," Tom told his wife. "He mentioned that he was planning to meet his friend Mark this morning – you know, the literary agent? They were going to meet in Lower Manhattan. James was hoping Mark could help him publish his book."

Helen shook her head disapprovingly at the thought of her brother's atheistic views. "I knew that his book, that '*Myth of Christianity*,' would be his downfall," she said with grief.

While Helen continued to watch the television, Danny joined her and leaned up against his mother. When the news report concluded, Tom mentioned that James had planned to leave for his appointment by 7:00 or 7:15 that morning.

"Maybe James is among the wounded," Helen said, kissing her son's forehead. She said goodbye to her husband, then picked up her cell phone and speed-dialed her brother. There was no response.

Helen didn't even realize she was crying until Danny asked, "Mommy, what's wrong?" Lifting him onto her lap and wrapping her arms around him tightly, she said, "Uncle James may be in trouble. We have to pray for him!"

11

LAURA O'MALLEY

MY PARALYSIS WAS only temporary as I lay in the morgue drawer. As soon as I could move again, I raised my hands in the total darkness and felt the cold metal inside the drawer above me and all around me.

I wept, wondering how long I would be trapped in the drawer. When I could no longer cry, I became desperate as I considered unending confinement in a tomb-like drawer, with all my mental abilities intact. This had to be the worst possible sentence. As a physician's assistant, I could easily imagine the most agonizing ways to die, but this made the most horrific deaths seem desirable.

With nowhere to go and only eternity to ponder the deep mysteries of life and death, I found myself thinking about God—a topic I suspected was forbidden in the antechamber of Hell.

Despite my fear of punishment, I folded my hands in prayer. The gesture brought instant warmth to my cold body. I cried out to the Lord, "Please, God, don't abandon me! Please save me!" The drawer began to open slowly. At first, I was intensely relieved, thinking that the Lord had heard my prayer. My relief changed to renewed terror as I was unexpectedly lifted from the drawer and levitated several feet above the tiled floor.

An instant later I was released and crashed to the ground. Just then the creature reappeared; he quickly confirmed my earlier suspicion that prayer would be punished here.

"Let's establish some ground rules, Laura. First, you must never invoke the name of my enemy again. Punishment will be swift and painful. Second, get it through your thick head that you've lost your chance for salvation. You're mine forever. If you're ever tempted to think about my enemy, it is in your best interest to remind yourself that you are a lost soul. If you ever again think that my enemy can help you or hear your disgusting pleas, consider these thoughts as temptations; you must resist them. You must try to please me—only me. I am your master. I can alleviate or increase your sufferings with a mere thought. Do you understand?"

I nodded.

"That's my little pumpkin. Unless you'd like to return to that drawer, I invite you to journey more deeply into my kingdom. That is the only way out of this tomb. Of course, this is with your permission."

I stared at him. "You don't have my permission! I want to leave your horrible kingdom, not go farther in!"

Satan hissed at me, then took a deep breath and exhaled toward me, the force of his breath throwing my body against the wall. His breath surrounded me, blasting me from all directions and slamming me into the walls again and again. Finally, I collapsed on the floor of the morgue, aching from the blows I had received.

"Get up," the creature growled. "For your insubordination, I commit you to the drawer for all eternity!"

I panicked as Satan laughed, "I have more interesting games to play with you while you're confined!"

I was promptly swept up and dropped into the drawer, which instantly slid closed. Helpless, I could only stare up at the familiar darkness. From somewhere outside, the creature laughed cruelly, "You should have accepted my invitation."

The words of the creature worked like poison in my heart. I knew for the first time what it meant to have absolutely no hope. However, what I discovered next as I trembled in the darkness gave me reason to doubt that all was truly lost.

12

KATHLEEN O'MALLEY

8:10 a.m.

KATHLEEN O'MALLEY, LAURA'S mother, was a recently retired high school teacher. She had just finished her rosary, and was sipping tea while watching the morning news. The local reporter on "Eye on the City," Sandra Sanchez-Pike, described a major explosion in one of Brooklyn's subway tunnels. The scene changed to show people emerging from the subway station, coughing and being assisted by medical personnel at the disaster site.

The camera focused again on Sanchez-Pike; she struggled to look composed as she reported the tragic story. "About an hour ago, a bomb was detonated on a Brooklyn N Train headed for Manhattan." Kathleen set down her tea with shaking hands, as she realized with a chill that her daughter must have been near the explosion. "The explosion took place in the tunnel between the Thirty-Sixth and Pacific Street stations. Authorities speculate that a suicide bomber was responsible for the explosion. Survivors from several compartments are beginning to exit from the tunnel. Wounded passengers are being transported to St. Alban's Hospital."

Then, touching her right hand to her hearing device, she added, "One compartment on the train was destroyed. No details have been given concerning the number of passengers who were injured or killed. Police and bomb squads are preparing to enter the tunnel to determine exactly what happened. Mayor Greenberg will make a statement about the alleged terrorist attack on the N Train. We'll be airing his statement, but first let's cut to the street above the subway station as we report this tragedy."

As the videographer moved away from Sanchez-Pike, the camera swept the crowd of frantic people who had escaped from the tunnel. Because of the soot and smoke blackening the faces of the survivors, it was impossible for Kathleen to tell if Laura was among them. When she didn't recognize her daughter in the crowd, she put her hand to her mouth to stifle her moans.

Some of the passengers who had been waiting for the N Train at the Pacific Street station were asked for their reactions to the blast. They expressed shock and grief over the many lives that were lost. One elderly man declared, "There's so much evil – I think the world is about to end!"

Kathleen reached for the phone and entered her daughter's cell phone number. Her face lit up when she heard Laura's voice, but then she realized that she was only listening to her daughter's voice mail message: "Hi, this is Laura. When you hear the beep, you know what to do!" She had no way of knowing that Laura had forgotten her cell phone at her apartment that morning.

Kathleen tried to speak calmly as she left a message. "Laura, honey, please call me right away when you get this message. I hope you weren't on the N Train headed for Manhattan this morning!"

After hanging up, she ran to the front door of their Long Island home to call her husband, Paul. He was removing snow from the driveway; the sound of the snow blower drowned out his wife's voice as she called him. With slippers on her feet, Kathleen ran outside in her bathrobe and stood in the snow, waving her hands above her head to attract her husband's attention. He turned off the snow blower and ran to her.

Paul took hold of his wife's shoulders. "What's going on?"

"Laura may be injured, or even worse! She had an interview for a new job this morning, and she was taking the N Train to Manhattan. A terrorist just blew up the train! I tried to call her cell phone, but I could only leave her a voicemail!"

13

Cathy Petersen

Cathy followed the creature down the train tunnel without a word. She admitted to herself that she had been a sinner. And yes, the relationship she had had with a married man was among the serious sins she was ashamed to admit. So was her abortion six weeks earlier.

Satan yanked Cathy by the wrist. "I can read your thoughts, my little dove. The fifth, sixth and ninth commandments are only starters! You have had little regard for my enemy's moral law. That delights me."

Despite the fact that her conscience accused her of sin, Cathy continued to doubt that she could be consigned to Hell forever.

Satan turned around to glare at her. "I'm going to take you to what my guests call the Lucifer Stadium. A short stay there should be enough to make you realize that there is no hope for you. I told you I am able to read your miserable thoughts. My stadium should cure you of the absurd notion that my enemy has any intention of saving your pitiful soul."

In an instant, Cathy found herself standing in a foul-smelling, muddy stadium littered with trash and filled with thousands of people of all ages, even some teenagers, walking in circles. They all cried, moaned or screamed, but they stopped momentarily to look at Cathy as she entered the stadium with Satan. Cathy shuddered as those around her genuflected in adoration of the beast and said with one voice, "Hail, Prince of Darkness." They rose and resumed their endless, circular march, abusing each other by pushing, shoving, hitting and spitting as they walked. Cathy turned and found that Satan had disappeared, leaving her to fend for herself.

Cathy tried to attract the attention of those passing nearest to her; she wanted desperately to communicate with someone. However, the unearthly voices only screamed louder each time she spoke. Whenever she made eye contact, the other person immediately shoved her away or slapped her face. Eventually she gave up and began to walk in circles also – or in whatever direction she was pushed. Unable to measure the passing of time, but feeling that she had been walking aimlessly for hours, Cathy moaned miserably like those around her, then screamed as she began to grasp the idea that this might be her eternity.

While Cathy cringed at her own blood-curdling screams, she was also repulsed by the bizarre noises made by the tormented souls around her; some barked, growled or clucked like chickens. A few of the teenagers even bleated like sheep.

Oddly, in the midst of the chaos assaulting her senses, Cathy found herself focused on that weird bleating. She was even more startled when her thoughts turned to the parable about the shepherd who went in search of the lost sheep. She recalled that the Good Shepherd, representing the Lord, left the ninety-nine sheep and searched until he found the one who had wandered away, placing it on his shoulders to carry it safely back to the fold.

"I am that lost sheep," Cathy perceived suddenly. Her hope renewed, she began to cry out within her soul, begging Christ to save her. She stopped screaming and felt peace enter into her soul. Satan must have been monitoring her; he returned to the stadium, yanked her by the hair and pulled her from the crowd.

"So you think my enemy will help you? You are *never* to think about my enemy or his blasphemous words! You refused to listen to him in life, and you will certainly not dwell on his words in death! Do you understand me, Cathy? You think your experience in this stadium is bad, but wait until I show you what I have in store for you now! Disobedience and blasphemy are not tolerated in my kingdom!"

In the blink of an eye, Cathy was standing next to Satan in a dim, muddy room that smelled of sewage and decayed flesh. "Welcome to your eternal dwelling place," the creature said as he threw her to the ground. "I think you'll need a little more light to appreciate your surroundings."

Mocking the Biblical creation story, Satan commanded, "Let there be light." Instead of sunlight, the red-orange glow intensified to reveal piles of corpses in various stages of decay scattered throughout the room. Once again, Satan disappeared.

Repulsed, Cathy stood for a moment among the putrid corpses before scurrying to an empty corner. Shaking and trying not to vomit, Cathy wept, but this time, she blocked all thoughts of sacred Scripture from her mind. She was totally focused on the horrific sights and odors around her. Even more, she was terrified that the beast would come back; her punishment might be even worse next time.

However, she soon realized that her fears must be feeding Satan and his minions – her terror was probably like a powerful narcotic for them. Cathy summoned all her strength, and forced herself to take a deep breath. Despite her fear of punishment, she dared to shut her eyes and envision herself as a little lost lamb awaiting the Good Shepherd.

If religious thoughts were so offensive to Satan, she hoped that they might be enough to expel her from his kingdom. She imagined Christ walking toward her, gently calling her name. When Cathy opened her eyes, she was no longer with the rotting corpses. The room was empty and clean, with a white light hovering above.

"Cathy, what have you done?" asked a voice emanating from the light.

"Is it you, Lord?"

"No. I am your guardian angel. I have been sent to you by the Lord." The angel showed the outline of his physical appearance to Cathy. The light streaming from the angel warmed her soul, and his presence filled her with consolation.

Despite the comfort she received, Cathy wondered if Satan or one his demons had come to her disguised as an angel of light. "That fiend told me that *he* was my guardian angel," she challenged him. "How do I know that you're telling the truth? How do I know that this is not a trick? Are you a fallen angel?"

"No. I come from the choir of guardian angels in Heaven. Although we do not have human names, you may find it helpful to refer to me as Uzziel. In Hebrew, this name means 'my power is God.' No fallen angel would claim such a name."

"Uzziel, what good is your visit to me now? I've sinned and I'm damned forever," Cathy burst out. "I thought I was saved, yet here I am in this pit of misery!"

"Yes, you were saved by the Lord, but the Lord never coerces," Uzziel explained. "The gift of salvation must be willingly accepted in time so that it may be celebrated in eternity."

Cathy stared at the soothing light and the outline of Uzziel. "So he was right! We can't be saved against our will."

"Correct. Lucifer is a fallen angel. He knows the truth. He has always known the truth and hated it. At the testing, he irrevocably opposed the Lord by an act of his will. He exalted himself and dared to claim superior status over the Creator. His foolish pride forever pitted him against God. Sadly, pride has brought you here to the antechamber of Hell. Cathy, admit to me what you have done."

Cathy lowered her head in shame and said, "I had an affair with a married man and became pregnant with his child."

"And?"

"I had an abortion six weeks ago. I really didn't want to do it, but I thought my relationship with Jason was worth the loss of our child."

With remorse and grief, Cathy explained her reason for being on the train. "I called Jason and planned to meet him at his law office today. He wanted proof that I had gone through with the abortion." She reached into her pocket for the envelope with the receipt, marked "Paid in Full" from Innovation Health Care Options, for her abortion.

"After I showed him the proof of my abortion, we were supposed to go to lunch and resume our relationship."

"Do you know where you are? Do you know what this place is?" asked Uzziel.

"I'm in Hell because of my sins," Cathy replied hopelessly.

"No. This is the *antechamber* of Hell. You still have a choice, but your contrition must be perfect."

Cathy looked up at the angel in amazement. "I've never heard of the *antechamber* of Hell. I know of Heaven and Hell, and you're either saved or damned. Do I really have a choice now? What is perfect contrition? I don't know what to think!"

"You're correct that Heaven and Hell are both permanent states. Since nothing impure can stand in the presence of God in his heavenly kingdom, God in his mercy has also provided a place of purification—a temporary state called Purgatory. Once purified, the soul is freed to enjoy the beatific vision."

Cathy listened attentively, then asked, "So this is like Purgatory?"

"No. The souls in Purgatory are already saved, and rejoice at their salvation, although they must suffer much to be purified of all defilement. The impediments to their union with God diminish as they unite their wills ever more perfectly to God's will. Their greatest agony is the delay of their ultimate union with the Almighty. You, Cathy, are in the *antechamber* of Hell. Here, souls make their final choice either to work out the salvation of their souls in fear and trembling or to choose eternal damnation. You are between life and death at this very instant. The final choice for salvation is always made before the moment of death."

"I'm not sure I understand," replied Cathy.

The angel continued, but this time without words. He communicated to Cathy's soul that between life and death, between time and eternity, while the soul is still in possession of its body, there is a fleeting second in which a soul comes to understand the gravity and depravity of sin. It is in this moment of clarity that the soul seals its eternal destination. The antechamber of Hell is not a place. Rather, it is a supernatural, mystical experience through which Evil is perceived and either accepted or rejected."

The angel concluded, using human language again, "You are passing from earthly life to eternal life. You are not yet dead. Very soon, your soul will separate from your body and your eternal fate will be sealed. God gives every opportunity for people to repent of their sins during their last days on Earth. In one final outpouring of God's mercy, some souls, like yours, linger a second in an unconscious state before the soul departs from the body. You are being given the opportunity to definitively choose life."

"But I was on the train that was blown up! Are you saying that I am still alive?"

"By human standards you appear dead, but God has not yet summoned your soul to judgment. You linger between two states of being, one that is temporal and the other that is eternal."

"I choose life! Get me out of here!" Cathy shouted.

"As I said, the antechamber of Hell is not a place. It is a spiritual experience. You don't 'get out' of the experience. You must *transcend it*," Uzziel replied.

"What does that mean? How do I transcend it?" asked Cathy.

Abruptly, she was transported back to the room with the putrefying cadavers around her.

"No, no! Come back!" Cathy cried out to Uzziel. "Don't abandon me to the creature of darkness!"

Satan reappeared and kicked the corpses as he approached her. "So I am the 'Creature of darkness!' How quaint! Did you enjoy your angelic illusion? I'm pretty talented, don't you think? You're very clever. I and my soldiers can appear as angels of light."

Cathy looked away from Satan and glanced at the spot where her angel had appeared. "My angel told me that I'm not damned forever. I still have a choice!"

"I was toying with you, my little dove. My hobby is to toy with souls. How does it feel to have your hopes crushed again? Part of the experience of Hell is the ongoing and unrelenting experience of despair. Abandon all hope."

Cathy refocused her gaze on Satan, doubts about her "angel" flooding her mind. She whispered hoarsely, "That wasn't Uzziel, my guardian angel? This was one of your tricks?"

"You're catching on, my little dove," Satan snarled as he turned toward the decaying corpses. Mocking the Lord's command to Lazarus, who was raised after being dead for three days, he ordered, "Come forth!" A decomposed corpse in the middle of the room struggled to its feet. Several other dead bodies began to rise and move toward Cathy. Although she knew it was entertaining to Satan, she was unable to keep from screaming. As he disappeared from the room, the beast hissed, "Enjoy your company, my little dove."

Six corpses extended their arms, reaching out to Cathy. She frantically searched the perimeter of the room for an escape route that did not exist.

14

DA'RELL THOMAS

As Da'rell listened to the demons fighting outside the cave, he heard one of them scolding the others, "We're just wasting time. The Master says we can do whatever we want to him."

His fear of what the demons would do to him, and the screams coming from the abyss only feet away, made Da'rell wish that he might experience a death that would put an end to all his suffering. He realized he had a choice to make. He could face the demons as they charged him or he could jump into the pit where crazed souls were screaming out of pure desperation. No matter which he chose, he knew that his suffering would never end.

For a split second, Tashira's face came to mind, momentarily suspending his decision. Everything around him vanished. He remembered how he loved Tashira, but didn't want to marry her. He recalled a conversation they had had earlier in the week.

"Marriage? Children?" cried Da'rell. "Baby, I send you to Planned Parenthood so we *don't* become parents! Why are you in such a rush to get married? We have a good thing going."

"No! *You* have a good thing going, Da'rell. Just for the record, I stopped taking the pill," Tashira had stated emphatically.

"What?"

"That's right. There are too many health risks with the pill. Just read the label!"

"Well, there are other forms of protection," he had replied, annoyed.

"I don't want protection. I want to be loved and respected. Before your grandma died, she said that if you refused to marry me, I should break up with you!"

"That sounds like something Grandma Pearl would say!" Da'rell remarked with resentment.

In the next instant, Da'rell saw his grandmother bathed in light only a few feet away from him in the cave. The light encompassed him and warmed his soul.

"I figured that you'd be here, Da'rell!"

"Are you here to torture me, Grandma Pearl? Did that creature send you? Those demons outside are ready to devour me!"

"Da'rell, the ole' Devil hates me. He despises me because I've received my eternal reward in God's kingdom. If you had listened to me in life, you wouldn't be here!"

Grandma Pearl had Da'rell's full attention. "The Devil and his demons can't hurt you as long as I'm with you. Now, let me get to the point of my visit! Boy, you did wrong by Tashira. After your poor mother died, I tried to raise you and your sister up right."

"Grandma, I know what you're going to say. You didn't like us living together, but I wasn't ready for marriage."

"What I liked or didn't like doesn't matter. It was God who was offended by your relationship with Tashira. Anyway, if you weren't ready for marriage, what were you ready for?" Shaking her head, Grandma Pearl continued, "So you weren't ready to get married, but you were ready to treat Tashira as your personal playground! Lust is such a nasty thing, Da'rell! Tashira deserves a *husband* who loves her and doesn't use her body like a thing!"

When Grandma Pearl finished scolding her grandson about the choices that he had made, including his decision to work for Planned Parenthood as a security guard, Da'rell replied in a remorseful tone, "You're right. You were always right!"

Then, as if afraid he had admitted too much, Da'rell attempted to rationalize his decision to avoid marriage. He blurted out, "Grandma Pearl, marriage is old-fashioned and doesn't work today. Fifty percent of all marriages end in divorce."

His grandmother shook a finger at her grandson. "You listen up! God's ways are not old-fashioned. *He* fashioned marriage and *He* makes the rules. I'm not here to debate with you about the reasons for the high divorce rate. No one thinks divorce is a good thing! Just ask the people who have had to endure it!"

Grandma Pearl put her hands on her hips. "I am here to tell you that Satan tells people that God's truth doesn't exist, and that Christian morality is old-fashioned. He wants people to create their own version of truth and morality, which is nothing more than a bunch of lies. You're here because your life was based on lies!"

Grandma went on to say that her grandson had substituted a religion that only worships pleasure for the Christian morals she had taught him. She pointed out that his employment at Planned Parenthood was especially foolish. "Do you realize you were supporting eugenics? Margaret Sanger despised black people and large families, and founding Planned Parenthood was part of her racist agenda."

For the first time since the explosion, Da'rell realized that he was in the antechamber of Hell because he had lived a selfish, arrogant and hedonistic lifestyle. The conscience he had ignored for years now convicted him.

Da'rell blurted out defensively, "Maybe I should have been gay!"

"Gay? Every person, made in the image and likeness of God, is called to be pure! The only moral sex is between a husband and wife—a man and a woman— as God intended it!"

Grandma Pearl continued, "What were you thinking

about this morning before the explosion? While you sat on the train, I saw you look at a photograph of Tashira and smile."

"I was thinking about how much I love Tashira. I thought of asking her to marry me."

"Well, there you are! For a split second, you were not being selfish. You wanted to change your ways. The good Lord is giving you a chance to change your destiny, even now."

"But there are no second chances in Hell."

"Da'rell, you're in the *antechamber* of Hell, not actually in Hell. You haven't appeared before the judgment seat of God yet. There's still time… "

"Time?"

"To accept salvation, but it won't be easy. The Devil *wants* you to despair! That's what the antechamber of Hell is all about—bringing souls to despair as they pass from life to death."

The light around Grandma Pearl began to fade.

"Don't go, Grandma! Stay!"

Complete darkness returned to the cave. Satan reappeared, enveloped in eerie, reddish-orange light, and a heavy sadness descended upon Da'rell's soul. "I do love to torment you, Da'rell. Did I get Grandma Pearl right, especially when she shook her finger at you?"

Da'rell was confused. Had it really only been Satan, toying with him?"

"You are here because you are supremely selfish and self-centered. You admitted it! That's what Hell is about. It's all about *you*. And lust is one of the best conduits to Hell. Do you know that I lusted after you all these years? Not in a sexual sense. I craved your soul, and now you're mine. You're my property!"

Da'rell shouted, "No! I don't belong to you!" Despite his defiant words, he felt hopeless again. As if reading his mind, Satan continued, "The antechamber of Hell is the reception area for lost souls. You are most certainly a lost soul. You were judged already, but since you were damned you will never have the memory of standing in my enemy's presence. That's my gift to you!" Satan snarled at him, evil gleaming in his eyes.

Satan watched Da'rell's response to his words, and perceived his doubts, then shouted gleefully, "Let the games continue." He disappeared, leaving Da'rell in darkness again.

The screams rose again from the great abyss. Demons, appearing as a hideous combination of beast and human being, entered the cave and encircled Da'rell. They paced around him, licking their lip and making guttural sounds, only occasionally uttering understandable words using human language. Most of the human words they used were blasphemies against the Lord of Heaven and Earth.

Responding to an unspoken command, five of the hideous creatures began to torment Da'rell by pushing him or swiping at him with their sharp claws. One had the body of a lion and the head of a man. Another had the body of a man and the head of a wolf. Two others looked like ferocious bears with deformed human faces. The last creature was the worst in appearance. It looked human, but its face was filled with rancid-smelling pustules, and its limbs were badly deformed. It opened its mouth, displaying decayed teeth. With spittle dripping from its mouth, the repulsive creature taunted Da'rell. "We look forward to torturing you! We hate you as much as the Master does."

The demonic creatures made a few false lunges at Da'rell to test his reaction. Da'rell glanced over at the abyss and made an impulsive decision to jump, screaming as he hurled himself off the ledge. Still screaming, he plunged downward into the darkness. Although he had been anxious to escape the demons in the cave, what he saw in the pit made him wish he hadn't jumped.

15

TASHIRA BOYD
8:10 a.m.

ALREADY DRESSED IN blue jeans and a blue tunic top, Tashira Boyd turned on the radio to her favorite Rhythm and Blues station. She turned up the volume and went into the bathroom. As she adjusted her intricately braided hair in front of the bathroom mirror, she heard the breaking news about the bomb on the N Train headed for Manhattan—the same train that Da'rell normally took to his job at Planned Parenthood.

Tashira reached for Da'rell's robe, from its hook on the back of the bathroom door. She lifted the sleeve of his robe to her face; she could still smell his familiar aftershave. Shocked, she worried that Da'rell had not gotten out of the train. As she was about to go into the living room to turn on the television, she was overcome with nausea.

Tashira knelt on the bathroom floor and vomited into the toilet. When she had finished, she sat on the floor and weakly propped herself up against the tiled bathroom wall. Earlier that morning, after Da'rell had left the apartment, Tashira had taken a pregnancy test and had confirmed that she was pregnant.

She dreaded Da'rell's reaction, fearing that he might suggest that she have an abortion at Planned Parenthood – a place that she had come to despise. Her younger sister, Jayla, just sixteen years old, had already had an abortion at one of their facilities. Following the abortion, she had become clinically depressed, and her stomach was pumped after taking an overdose of her mother's sleeping pills. Fortunately, her attempted suicide had failed, and she was now receiving counseling.

Guilt consumed Tashira as she considered her role in her sister's abortion. When Jayla had confessed to Tashira that she had become sexually active at age fifteen, she encouraged her little sister to go to Planned Parenthood for birth control pills. Within the year, when Jayla became pregnant, Tashira had encouraged her to terminate the pregnancy. Following the abortion, Jayla's life began to unravel and spin out of control. When Tashira realized that it was the abortion that had caused her little sister's depression and attempted suicide, she changed her thinking on Planned Parenthood and abortion.

Now that Tashira was pregnant, she intended to turn her life around and be the best mother that she could be to her baby. She intended to tell Da'rell that night that she wanted to get married. Their baby deserved a mother and father committed to each other for life.

Tashira gently placed her hand on her abdomen. "No one is going to take you away from me!" Then it occurred to her that the baby growing in her womb might never see Da'rell.

16

James Simonelli, Ph.D.

JAMES OPENED HIS eyes and glanced at the ground, splattered with blood from his scourging. His wrists were bruised from the rope that bound him to the stone pillar. He slumped forward, lacking the strength to stand erect. Strangely enough, he remembered a line from the Scriptures, "By his wounds you were healed." He mused that his own wounds had no value beyond reminding him of the senseless torture he had just endured.

Each time he tried to stand, he could feel the raw flesh on his back tear open. The agony was almost unbearable. James heard a voice say to him, "Resist him." The voice repeated, "Resist him. By his wounds you were healed. Now accept that healing."

"Who are you? Let me see you!" James demanded, with all the strength he could muster.

The ropes binding his wrists loosened and his hands were freed. Too weak to stand, James clung to the stone pillar and dropped to his knees. A bright white light appeared, and he saw an angelic figure standing only a few feet away. His eyes had become accustomed to the dull orange glow; now the bright light caused him to squint. He asked again, "Who are you?"

The figure responded, "I am your guardian angel, James. I am here to help you find your way home."

"You're my angel? Do you have a name?"

"You may call me Ariel. In Hebrew my name means 'Lion of God.' You are in the *antechamber* of Hell. Listen to me if you wish to be saved."

The angel raised his arm, wielding an invisible force that helped James to his feet. Then the angel instructed James to think about his teenage years. "Do you remember the path you took so long ago that led you away from the Lion of Judah?"

James recalled from his former extensive studies of the Bible that the "Lion of Judah" represented Jesus Christ. He focused on the events and decisions that had led him to renounce his Catholic faith and the Lord Himself.

In silence, James called to mind his refusal, during his freshman year in high school, to attend classes to prepare for the sacrament of Confirmation. Each week he had battled with his parents and insisted that they allow him to "follow his conscience." He told his parents that he wasn't sure what he believed, arguing that they had no right to force their Catholic faith on him.

His parents were horrified by their son's rebellion and pleaded with James to stay in the Confirmation program. When he had refused to cooperate, they reluctantly allowed him to withdraw from religion classes. However, that was only the first stage of his apostasy.

Several weeks later, he told his parents that he would no longer go to Mass with them on Sundays. He claimed that he no longer believed that the Eucharist was the body, blood, soul and divinity of Christ. He told them that he found the Mass boring and of no value.

His parents assumed that denying privileges and punishing their son would eventually force him to come to his senses and repent. Instead, he persistently defied his parents' orders for him to accompany them to Mass.

Totally frustrated with their son's behavior and their constant battles with him over their beliefs and values, his parents relented and allowed James to pursue his sinful behavior. Helpless, they prayed fervently that their son's adolescent rebellion would be short-lived.

When James opened his eyes at last, the angel was no longer visible to him. He could hear the angel's final words, though, and they echoed in his mind, "Believe in the Lion of Judah and resist the beast with all your will."

James cried out, "I believe! I believe!"

As the white light disappeared, Satan reappeared and stood before James, dressed in a black tuxedo.

"I'm so talented that I can take on the appearance of an angel of light. I did this to make you review at least one of the decisions in your life that brought you to my kingdom. Once you resign yourself to the fact that you are lost for all eternity, the real agony will begin. That's what Hell is all about — eternal and relentless agony."

As though pierced with a sword, James yelled, "You're a liar! I told the angel that I believed in Christ. This is only the antechamber of Hell. I'm not damned yet!"

"You may believe in my enemy's existence, but you will never see him or experience his presence. You, my dear James, are among the damned! Now I will introduce you to even more excruciating pains, since you again blasphemed by referring directly to my enemy."

Satan clapped his hands several times, and James was sent to a dungeon containing a huge pyre of burning wood. The flames were at least ten feet high. No matter where James moved in the dungeon, the heat was so intense that his wounds sizzled. Satan stood close to the flames.

"James, this isn't the type of fire associated with Pentecost Sunday! But then, you never did complete your catechism lessons on Confirmation. You were a rebellious lad!" Satan said sarcastically. Motioning to James to follow him into the fire,

Satan added, "I'm not afraid of the flames. Why not join me?" The beast walked into the flames untouched, then vanished.

Alone, in extreme pain and weak from the scourging, James leaned against one of the dungeon walls, but the heat made his wounds almost unbearable. The agony was unlike anything he had experienced in life. Despite it all, James folded his hands in prayer and begged Ariel to assist him.

"That's right, James. Pray," he heard his angel say.

As he prayed, the flames around him became gradually less intense, and his wounds began to heal. In an instant, he was transported out of the dungeon, and found himself in the bedroom that he had occupied in his childhood home. He spotted his old baseball bat in the corner, picked it up, and stroked the familiar chip at the top. Shaking his head, he wondered how he could be back in his bedroom. He glanced at the mirror, still hanging above the same old dresser. Surprised to see his face reflected as an adolescent, he tossed his bat on the bed and lifted his T-shirt to see if he had scars from the scourging and fire. His young body was unscathed.

As he tried to make sense out of what had happened to him, he heard Martha Simonelli calling him from the hallway. As soon as he heard his mother's voice, he understood that he was about to relive one of the worst days of his life. He could not see his angel, but Ariel's voice confirmed, "You will relive a few moments of your life, but you will not be able to change anything."

As he had done so long ago, James walked to the door and opened it a few inches. He saw his parents coming down the hallway with his four-year-old sister, Helen. His baby brother, Tommy, only two years old, had been diagnosed with acute leukemia several days earlier. He had been placed in intensive care at St. Mary's Children's Hospital in New York.

Robert Simonelli, his father, delivered the heart-wrenching news to James in his bedroom. "Your baby brother's battle with cancer is over. Tommy passed away a couple of hours ago in my arms."

James cried out, "Tommy is dead? It's not fair!"

"Life is not fair," his mother murmured, wiping her eyes.

His father hugged him, but James tried to pull away. Robert insisted, "We're people of faith, James. Someday we'll see Tommy again in heaven."

"That's not good enough for me!" James cried.

He stormed out of his bedroom and went into the bedroom Tommy had shared with Helen. There, in his brother's crib, were several of his favorite stuffed animals. For a moment, he held the giraffe, Tommy's favorite toy, in his arms. Then, in anger, he threw the stuffed giraffe against the wall.

"I don't believe in a God who would take the life of a baby!" James shouted.

He didn't realize that his mother had followed him into the bedroom. "James, please don't say such things. Tommy is with God now. If it weren't for God, I don't think I could handle my grief."

James turned to his mother and put his arm around her shoulders as she buried her face in his T-shirt. He closed his eyes and held his mother silently, knowing that he could only add to her grief by denying the existence of the God. When he opened his eyes, it was four years later, and he stood in a funeral parlor looking down at his mother's body in her casket. Martha Simonelli had died just months after being diagnosed with the pancreatic cancer that spread aggressively throughout her body.

James looked away from his mother's emaciated body and sat down next to his sister Helen, who was now eight. His father stood near their mother's casket, greeting the many friends and family members who had come to pay their respects.

When his father told him of his mother's death, James had wanted to shout to his father that this was his father's reward for being a Christian. But James held back his words because his father embraced him and said that he needed James more than ever. James decided that day that he would never allow himself to need anyone in his life.

At the time of his mother's death, James was eighteen and about to begin college; he had been accepted as a scholarship student at Princeton University. Within weeks, he intended to leave home and begin his studies. He told himself then that one day he would publish a book exposing belief in God as a myth. Right now, though, he stared at his mother's lifeless body and reminded himself that he would never see her again.

In the blink of his eye, James found himself at his mother's funeral Mass at St. Augustine Church. He looked around and marveled that so many people clung to the belief in the immortal soul. He felt liberated as he rejected their belief in an omnipotent God or an eternal afterlife.

However, James' elation melted into profound emptiness as the priest preached about eternal life and the rewards of Heaven for those who persevere in their lives of faith, and he wanted desperately to flee from the church. James remained in his pew, not because he believed, but for the sake of his little sister. Helen had taken hold firmly of his arm and placed her cheek against his shoulder. He turned to his little sister and lied, "Everything is going to be all right. Mommy is in a better place now."

Helen looked up at her big brother. "You won't leave me, will you?"

James smiled at his sister. "Never," he agreed, knowing that within two months he would move to Princeton.

At the end of Mass, James, his father and several other men in the family stood up to accompany Martha's casket down the center aisle. As her casket was placed in the hearse, James turned for a last look at the sanctuary of the church. He vowed never to set foot in another church building as long as he lived. Moreover, he would become the best atheist that had ever lived.

With that memory fresh in his mind, James found himself back in the darkened dungeon; ashes littered the dirt floor where the fire had blazed earlier. James' wounds had partially healed, but the burns on his feet were still blistered and painful. Every inch of his body ached. The incredible thing about the antechamber of Hell was that no matter what kind of pain or physical torture was inflicted, the body seemed to absorb it and heal, only to be ready for more abuse. James wondered what torment was in store for him next.

Satan reappeared, asking, "What have you been doing?"

James realized that Satan had no idea where he had been, so he stood his ground and said nothing.

"Cat got your tongue, James?" the creature asked nervously.

With great effort, James folded his arms across his aching chest.

"I command you to speak, James. What are you thinking?"

The creature couldn't read his mind. For the first time in decades, James began to feel a sense of hope.

17

CATHY PETERSEN

LIKE ZOMBIES IN a horror movie, three hideous, decomposing corpses reached for Cathy. She barely escaped their grasp as she dashed toward the far end of the room, crying out to her guardian angel, "Uzziel, help me!"

Just as one of the corpses was about to touch Cathy's arm, she backed up against one of the walls and passed through it as light passes through a window pane. On the other side of the wall, she found herself in a secluded, wooded area. Without hesitation, she ran beyond the trees and stood in a meadow that was bathed in natural sunlight. Delighted, she felt the warmth of the sun on her face, feeling wonderfully alive and grateful. Uzziel had rescued her from the zombies.

Several yards away, Cathy could hear water flowing down a stream where dozens of children were wading. They were accompanied by their own angels, who were giving them instructions.

Cathy rejoiced at hearing birds singing in the bushes and nearby trees; breathing deeply, she could smell the flowers that dotted the landscape. Where was she, and what was happening to her? She heard music in the background – a merry-go-round?

Uzziel appeared beside her. "Why did you doubt, Cathy? Did I not tell you that the antechamber of Hell is a spiritual experience? Did I not say that you have to transcend it?" the angel asked sternly.

"There were…dead people…coming after me! The smell…I couldn't think straight, or remember what you had said. I was terrified!"

"The only thing that should frighten you is eternal damnation."

Uzziel turned his gaze to the children wading in the stream. "What's happening to those children?" asked Cathy.

"They are being reborn to love," explained Uzziel.

Cathy reflected on the angel's words. She herself felt incapable of real love, as though that part of her had slipped into a vacuum. Her only emotions since she had entered the antechamber of Hell were dread and fear. She admitted to Uzziel that it seemed impossible for her even to contemplate faith or love in the midst of such grotesque horrors. "You must learn to love in the midst of the horrors. Love is an act of the will. Faith is a decision," Uzziel emphasized.

"But *how* do I find faith and love in the midst of such awful…?" Cathy's voice trailed off; she was unable to find words to describe what she had experienced.

"You must exercise your faith in the same way any person must exercise faith and love during the trials and tribulations in the world. In the antechamber of Hell, trials and tribulations take on horrific and diabolical dimensions. They reflect the depths to which you sank in your spiritual life on earth. You must see beyond the horrors and keep your will focused on God, and then you must dwell in his love," Uzziel responded.

Cathy tried to understand the angel's advice. "Right now, your fear of the beast and his punishment far exceeds the love that you profess for God. Your love must be perfected in this brief passage from temporal to eternal life. Above all, you must truly convert and repent of your sins."

Without warning, Cathy found herself in the lobby of a

downtown Brooklyn office building, on the day when she had noticed Jason for the first time.

She heard Uzziel's voice within her. "You will relive your past, but you will be unable to change anything."

Jason Hall was waiting for the elevator in the lobby that morning when Cathy caught him gazing at her. Her eyes met his, and they both looked away, but moments later she found herself discreetly studying the handsome business attorney. With approval she noted that his brown, wavy hair was well-styled and his light green eyes seemed to sparkle.

"I assume you work in this building," he said with a smile.

"Yes. I was hired two weeks ago as the accounts receivable clerk at T.R. Wright Insurance Brokers. Fifteenth floor."

Shifting his briefcase from his right hand to his left, Jason leaned over to shake Cathy's hand cordially. "I've noticed you here at this elevator the past few mornings. I'm Jason Hall, an attorney for Bender, Grayson and Dodd on the ninth floor."

Cathy was flattered that Jason had noticed her. She glanced down at Jason's left hand; no wedding ring. It was Cathy's turn to smile.

In the elevator, he asked, "Would you be interested in having lunch with me at that pub down the block one of these days?"

Without hesitation, Cathy replied, "I'd like that."

Jason winked playfully as he got off the elevator. "I know where to find you!"

The next scene Cathy relived was the following week. She was sitting in a booth at the pub with Jason, as they ordered their salads. That's when she had noticed a gold wedding ring on Jason's left hand.

"I thought you were single," Cathy said, alarmed.

"Technically, I am married. Barbara and I are talking about a separation and divorce within the year. I still care for her. She's the mother of our three children," Jason told her without a hint of emotion.

"You have three children?"

"Yes. One is seven and the twins are three."

"I agreed to have lunch with you because I thought you were single. You weren't wearing a wedding band when you introduced yourself in the lobby!"

"I'm a lawyer, Cathy. Divorce is merely the final legal step in a relationship that has failed miserably. It's a legal maneuver to protect assets and make civil any custody issues. Divorce doesn't end a marriage. That usually happens months and sometimes years before any legal action is taken in a court of law. My marriage to Barbara has been over since the twins were born."

Jason had argued his point well, thought Cathy. His marriage was over and the divorce was just a legal formality. She wondered what had made their marriage fall apart.

"If the marriage is over, why are you wearing your wedding ring?" asked Cathy.

"Barbara insisted that we go for marriage counseling before finalizing our legal separation. She said that she wanted us to make every attempt to mend our broken marriage. The truth is that the marriage is beyond repair. I put the ring back on last week to show that our marriage did mean something to me—at least enough to go to counseling. I guess I forgot to take it off. We are going forward with the divorce sooner rather than later."

He removed the band from his finger and put it in his vest pocket. "The marriage is over. Honest."

"Are you absolutely sure?"

"Absolutely. Barbara and I agreed that we care enough about each other not to drag things out. I'm moving into a studio apartment as soon as I can find one in downtown Brooklyn. Barbara and the kids will keep our Long Island home."

"Don't you feel that dating me would be at all inappropriate during your separation?"

"No! First of all, I'm not looking to get into a serious relationship with you. Can't we just be friends and have lunch together?"

Cathy was disarmed by Jason's words.

"Sure, we can be friends," she replied.

Cathy remembered now that she had felt a coldness enter her body at that moment; she reached for her sweater and wrapped it around her shoulders. What Cathy realized now was that Satan was a third party at the table that afternoon. Though she had not realized it at the time, his presence had chilled her.

Just as the waitress brought a tray with their salads and drinks, a stunning brunette in her thirties passed their table and paused, obviously recognizing Jason. She waited until the waitress finished, then ignored Cathy and glared down at Jason. Clutching her handbag, she said tensely, "I thought you were going to call me!"

Jason cleared his throat, apparently shocked to see the woman. He excused himself from the table and steered her over to the bar. Whatever he said seemed to have a calming effect at first, but when he placed his hand on her shoulder, the brunette brushed it off and left the pub. Jason returned to the table with a smile.

"I'm sorry for the intrusion. That was a disgruntled client. I had to assure her that we have her best interests in mind in a court case."

What Cathy didn't know at the time was that Claudette Powell was not a client at all. She was having an affair with Jason – an affair that he intended to end as quickly as possible.

After lunch, Cathy and Jason strolled back to the office building together.

"I'd like to take you to lunch next Friday," Jason said.

Although Cathy felt some discomfort about Jason's marital status, she convinced herself that a few casual lunch dates with him could not do any harm. She accepted his invitation. Their lunches soon progressed into real dates, which evolved into a romantic affair that led to the conception of their child.

As Cathy relived their luncheon dates, she saw that a relationship with Jason could never have fit into God's plan for her.

Jason was an unfaithful husband and an expert in deception. His numerous extramarital affairs in the course of four years had proven that he had no regard for the vows he had made to Barbara. Divorced or not, God considered Jason off limits for Cathy.

Again, Uzziel addressed Cathy. "Your sinful affair with Jason led to the conception of your daughter."

The angel's words pierced Cathy's heart. She never wanted to think about her unborn child, but had always suspected that the baby she aborted was a girl.

The next episode that Cathy relived was at a Japanese restaurant. By this time, Jason had moved out of his studio apartment and back to the Long Island house he had shared with Barbara and their children. Jason was explaining to Cathy that his original plan to divorce Barbara within the year was unrealistic.

"We've agreed to stay together for the sake of the children," he said, avoiding eye contact. Cathy had invested so much in her relationship with Jason that she readily accepted his lies – he claimed that he and Barbara slept in separate bedrooms, with no intimacy. He also played on her emotions by suggesting that had moved back home mainly because Barbara needed his help; she was unable to handle their autistic son and his recent behavioral problems by herself.

Despite Cathy's humiliation at being Jason's mistress, she accepted the conditions for their ongoing affair rather than lose him. They could continue as a "couple" as long as Cathy consented to remain discreet about their relationship.

Jason was quite satisfied with his arrangement with Cathy for several months. Now, Cathy relived that afternoon in Jason's law office when she announced that she was pregnant, several months after Jason had moved back to the home he shared with Barbara.

"You're pregnant? You have to get an abortion!"

"Divorce Barbara and marry me! We can raise our child together. Staying with Barbara is just insane! You've told me again and again that you don't love her!"

"You're right. I don't love her." Jason paced back and forth in his office. "But if she ever learned about our affair and the baby, she would file for divorce right away." Jason paused and laid both hands gently on her shoulders. "I told you that my wife comes from a very wealthy family. Her father, the Grayson in Bender, Grayson and Dodd, is backing me financially in a real estate business venture. I need his help. Do you understand?"

Cathy removed his hands from her shoulders. Then she said, with clenched teeth, "So it's all about money! But I'm carrying your child …"

"It's not a child yet!" Jason responded with annoyance.

"How would you characterize our relationship, Jason? Is it merely convenient and casual sex?" she asked. Then, placing her right hand on her abdomen, she looked at him. "If this is not a child, then what is it?"

Jason shook his head from side to side. He had no intention of debating with Cathy about the beginning of human life. "You know that I love you, but I can't get a divorce right now. Anyway, your pregnancy was unplanned. It was a mistake. We can't bring an unwanted child into the world."

"So this child is nothing more than a mistake that we made?" she asked, blinking back tears.

Lifting a metal box from his desk drawer, Jason pulled out a white envelope filled with cash, and counted ten one hundred dollar bills. "This should more than take care of your expenses for the procedure. Afterwards, treat yourself to a manicure, pedicure or whatever else will make you feel better."

Jason looked at Cathy and repeated calmly, "Yes, this child is a mistake. I'm sorry this is so difficult for you, but we have no choice." He pressed the money into Cathy's palm, but she pushed his hand away, objecting, "I don't want your money, Jason."

Again, Jason tried to hand the money to Cathy. Defiantly, she withdrew her hand from his, and the bills fell to the floor between them. Jason bent to pick them up, saying slowly and with emphasis, "I know you think that you want this child, but you'll see that I'm right."

Holding the money out to her, Jason added, "There's a place called Innovation Health Care Options in Lower Manhattan. It's a state-of-the-art reproductive service center. You can have the abortion there."

What Cathy didn't know was that the brunette named Claudette Powell, the woman that Jason had identified as a "client," had also conceived his child and then had an abortion at Innovation Health Care Options. Jason had ended their relationship when Claudette refused to remain Jason's "secret partner." It was Claudette's telephone call to Jason's wife that had led to their first separation.

Jason held up the money like a fan in his left hand, and lightly touched Cathy's shoulder with his right, then ran his hand down her arm to take her hand. Once more he placed the money in the palm of her hand. "Cathy, it's going to be all right. I don't think it's wise for me to be seen with you when you go for the abortion. Ask one of your friends to go with you. We can talk on the phone daily."

Almost as an afterthought, Jason added, "After the abortion, in about six weeks, we can get together as usual. Maybe we can even escape for a weekend and fly down to Florida soon. What do you think? I don't want to lose you, Cathy." Cathy was angry, hurt and confused all at the same time. She wished that she could hate Jason, but she simply couldn't. The price she would have to pay for their relationship was the abortion. When Jason insisted that she show him the receipt for the abortion, she knew that he was absolutely serious about wanting her pregnancy terminated.

Sympathetically, Jason added, "I'm truly sorry that the pregnancy complicated things for us. We'll have to be very careful in the future; we have to be smart. One of these days, I will divorce Barbara. I want you to be the next Mrs. Hall."

Cathy nodded and clung to the idea that she would marry Jason in the future.

Jason held Cathy in his arms. "Everything is going to be fine. We'll be fine. You have to trust me. You are doing the right thing for us."

When their conversation ended, Jason kissed Cathy tenderly as though nothing had happened.

Cathy left Jason's office, relieved that their relationship had not ended. Then a depressing thought entered her mind as she stood waiting for the elevator. She wondered if she was carrying a male or female child.

The doors to the elevator disappeared. Again, Uzziel stood beside Cathy in the woods. "You had an affair with a married man – an extremely selfish married man – you conceived a child whom you destroyed in order to maintain the relationship. You silenced your conscience again and again. You allowed your unruly passions to dominate and suppress all reason. Deep down, you knew the truth, but tried to bury it. God's truth can never be buried!"

Uzziel asked Cathy to explain what she had planned to do on the day of the explosion. Cathy admitted that she was to meet Jason downtown and show him the receipt for the abortion. She had been so angry after the abortion that at first she refused to show it to him during their weekly luncheon dates. Since more than a month had passed, she knew that Jason would soon end their relationship unless she assured him that she had aborted the child.

Uzziel inquired, "Were you having a change of heart this morning about resuming your relationship with Jason?"

"Yes," admitted Cathy. "I was conflicted. I hadn't slept all night. I thought I loved and needed Jason in order to be happy, but the overwhelming guilt about the abortion had changed everything. It changed me. I kept thinking about the baby –

the baby that I had sacrificed for Jason. The more I thought about the abortion, the more I resented Jason and hated myself. I wanted to give him the receipt for my abortion and announce that the price of his affection was too high. I wanted to tell him that I was meant to be a wife and not a mistress or concubine. At least, that's what I thought I might do."

Suddenly, Cathy found herself in the empty lobby of Innovation Health Care Options. Afraid to move even a muscle, she heard a young child singing, "Mary had a little lamb, little lamb, little lamb; Mary had a little lamb; its fleece was white as snow." The little girl, no more than four years old, skipped into the lobby. She stood perfectly still as Cathy studied her features. Without a doubt, the child looked like Jason Hall. She had his curly brown hair and light green eyes.

"Who are you?" Cathy asked.

The little girl smiled and then giggled, "My name is Angelica because the angels named me! I'm your daughter."

"No. This can't be happening. I … I aborted you! Have you been sent here to torture me?"

"I came to help you find your way home, Mommy. Uzziel said you needed my help."

Cathy didn't know what to think or how to act. She was in shock, overwhelmed with grief and remorse. Angelica approached Cathy and took her hand.

"Don't cry, Mommy. I'm here!"

Cathy dropped to her knees to look into Angelica's eyes. She repeated over and over, "I'm so sorry. Please forgive me, Angelica."

Angelica hugged her mother tightly. "You're forgiven, Mommy," she said with a big smile.

Then Angelica spoke to Cathy with the maturity of an adult. "This is how God loves and forgives. His love and forgiveness is most pure and simple."

18

DA'RELL THOMAS

D A'RELL LEAPED INTO the dark pit to avoid the demons, and tumbled onto a pile of bodies that cushioned his fall. There was just enough red-orange light to see that the bodies were charred. Repulsed, Da'rell jumped off the pile of corpses and fell to the ground.

Looking around, Da'rell saw that he was at the end of an area about the size of a football field. Hundreds of charred bodies, the walking dead, were lined up like soldiers in formation. They marched barefoot across the burning embers which covered the field. When they reached the opposite end, they reconfigured their ranks along the sidelines to continue their never-ending, torturous trek across the embers. Their pain must have been excruciating; it was their agonized cries that he had heard from the cave above. He looked down at his own bare feet and understood that he would soon be tortured in the same way.

Satan greeted Da'rell cheerfully, "I guess anyone would have chosen to jump rather than be eaten alive by my demons. At any rate, wherever you are in my kingdom, the pain is real, intense and never ending! Join the walkers," Satan ordered.

Without moving, the beast thrust Da'rell into the midst of the crowd that began yet another trek across the sizzling field.

"Don't let that imaginary conversation with your grandmother fool you. You are in Hell. Enjoy your exercise!" Satan departed like a puff of smoke.

The smell of burning flesh surrounded Da'rell as he walked beside the charred bodies into the field of burning embers. The pain was unbearable as his own feet began to blister and burn. With each step, he screamed in agony; he expected to pass out from the pain, but he was unable to stop walking or to lose consciousness. The only relief for him and his companions was when they reached the ends of the field. Their burned flesh then healed enough so they could continue their fruitless march. Eventually, Da'rell glanced back at the charred bodies that had broken his fall; they were moving slightly. With a shudder, he guessed that they had been forced to walk through flames. Was that the next torture that Satan planned for him?

Though he feared Satan's retribution, Da'rell cried out, "Lord, please save me!" As soon as he completed his prayer, Da'rell found himself in a beautiful garden with a white marble fountain. Water streamed into the fountain from a golden pitcher suspended in the air above it.

A voice said, "Put your feet and legs in the healing water, Da'rell."

Da'rell obediently sat on the edge of the fountain. The cool water soothed, healed and refreshed his feet. The pain in his feet and legs vanished.

Grandma Pearl appeared by the fountain dressed in what she had always called her "Easter best;" her favorite pink dress, a string of pearls, and a large straw hat adorned with colorful flowers. "Grandma, is it really you? Or is this another trick?" "What's the matter with you, Da'rell? Why did you doubt that I came to you the first time? Can't you see, he wants you to despair! If the devil was impersonating me, would he have spoken to you as I did?"

"I thought he was just tormenting me."

"Jesus loves you and wants you to be saved. Would that rascal say such a thing? Use your head and smarten up!"

Da'rell shook his head. "It really is you, Grandma Pearl! I don't think the devil would ever say the name of Jesus."

"Then know that you're not in Hell. As I told you, you are in the antechamber of Hell. That means you are about to pass from life to death, from time to eternity. Our good Lord gives us every opportunity to repent of our sins, even if it's in the final second of life. That split second before your soul passes out of its bodily temple can seem like days or years in the antechamber of Hell. The truth is that you are about to die."

"So what do I need to do to be saved?"

"You must want to do God's will perfectly."

"But I'm imperfect—a sinner," Da'rell lamented. "You pointed that out to me!"

"That's true, but you can, with an act of your will, love God and the things of God perfectly. In your final second, you must submit your soul to God's will with perfect love. The Lord came to Earth to call the sinners, not the righteous ones."

"I've been a failure up until now. How can I possibly love perfectly?"

"Listen up and don't make me say things twice. The beast is searching for you. God will permit him to summon you only after I have spoken the truth to you. The beast doesn't have unrestrained power over you or anyone else, even in the antechamber of Hell. Your guardian angel is looking out for you. You will make his acquaintance shortly. Remember that in order to submit your soul to God you have to want to conform your will to his will in all things."

Da'rell tried to grasp his grandmother's words. Her image became more and more opaque until she disappeared. Her last words to him were, "Don't let the beast confuse you. He was a liar from the beginning. Don't listen to him. He has nothing of value to say to you. Resist him with all your will. Elior, your guardian angel, will instruct you. Listen to him." The garden and everything in it disappeared. Da'rell found himself once again standing in the presence of Satan.

Now the beast looked ravenous. His once handsome features were now anything but attractive. His face was contorted with rage. As Satan opened his mouth to speak, Da'rell smelled his foul breath. He addressed Da'rell in a sinister tone, "Well, Da'rell. Grandma Pearl did make her way back to you again! But it was all for nought! Do you know why?" Da'rell refused to respond to the beast, as Grandma Pearl had advised him.

"I'll tell you why! Because I have you where I want you in the antechamber of Hell. What makes you think that you will be saved in an instant when you've made all the wrong choices during your whole miserable life? Did your grandmother tell you that many souls pass through the antechamber of Hell and never make it to my enemy's kingdom? They stay with me and my legion forever!"

Da'rell looked up, surprised by the beast's revelation. Once Satan had Da'rell's attention, he fine-tuned his temptation. "That's right, Da'rell. Throughout time, millions of souls have been sent to the antechamber of Hell, and not one of them ever exited to my enemy's realm. Your dear grandmother was simply describing the theoretical. It is possible for a soul to escape from the antechamber, but it is highly improbable that it will."

Da'rell began to doubt Grandma Pearl's words. However, this time he remained silent.

The beast licked his lips with his forked tongue as he studied Da'rell's face. "Let me repeat, no one has ever escaped from the antechamber of Hell. All the souls descended to the lower regions of Hell. Do you know why?"

Da'rell again met Satan's question with silence.

"It's because they are unable to love perfectly and embrace my enemy's will totally! Do you really think that you are capable of perfect love or doing the will of my enemy in all things?"

The creature watched again for the slightest reaction from Da'rell. When he saw Da'rell flinch at his words, he continued to chip away at his hope for salvation.

With greater eagerness and cunning, the creature continued, "You are here because you did your will in the world. I don't condemn you for that! In my kingdom, that's laudable! What was so bad about you and Tashira living together? What value is a piece of paper when two people are attracted to each other? Carnal desires are meant to be satisfied. Why else would my enemy have given them to you? He has no regard for peoples' feelings and needs! Once you leave the antechamber of Hell, I promise you all kinds of carnal delights!"

With that last statement, Da'rell realized that Satan was again toying with him. Judging by his experience so far, it was obvious that nothing pleasant awaited those in Satan's kingdom. Again, he recalled the advice that his grandmother had given moments earlier, "Remember, the beast has nothing of value to say. He's a liar. He was a liar from the beginning."

"Da'rell, what are you thinking now? I don't like it when I can't tell what's on your mind. There is punishment for such noncompliance!"

The beast muttered something, and he and Da'rell were standing in a dungeon with bones strewn on the ground around them. Satan smiled. "I had the flesh melted from their miserable skeletons for their insubordination! I think you need another lesson about my power!" Da'rell was abruptly suspended about fifteen feet in the air, dangling by a chain around his wrists over a giant boiling cauldron in the middle of the room. "If you wish to shield your thoughts from me, behold what I have in store for you!"

Satan continued lightheartedly, "I pull out all the stops here. I'll give you the experience of a lifetime, or rather, after-lifetime. If you thought walking on hot embers was painful, wait until you are lowered into the boiling water inch by inch. You will be fully immersed. We'll call it a baptism of desire for eternal life with me in Hell."

Satan vanished, leaving Da'rell still hanging over the cauldron. His weight tore the skin from his wrists and strained his arm and shoulder muscles. Slowly, the chain lowered him from the blackness above toward the bubbling pool below. Soon he was close enough to feel the heat and smell the water; it was filthy and foul.

Satan's voice rang out, "This baptism cancels your first one! If you cry out to your grandmother or the enemy again, you'll boil for all eternity!"

With no possible escape from the boiling cauldron, Da'rell dared to cry out, "Please, God, save me! Help me to accomplish your will perfectly, even here!"

19

Laura O'Malley

I T SEEMED AS though I had been trapped in the drawer of the morgue, cramped and terrified, for weeks. As I stared into the blackness that surrounded me, the thought of being entombed alone forever left me longing for unconsciousness or death.

As I considered eternal damnation, its horror brought me to the brink of despair. I pounded on the sides of the locked drawer until my knuckles were bloody. I am not sure what I was hoping for or expecting, but what happened next was the most extraordinary gift God has ever given me. I saw my mother at home in her rocking chair, with her Rosary in her hand. As she began the last mystery, I silently mouthed the familiar prayers of my childhood with her. By the end of the decade, I found enough courage to pray the Hail, Holy Queen aloud, clasping my hands together over my chest and begging the Lord to save me.

Incredibly, I was no longer trapped in the morgue drawer! To my delight, I found myself in an open field with wildflowers blooming all around. In the distance, I saw young children riding solid gold horses on a merry-go-round; their laughter mingled with the joyful music. As much as I wanted to celebrate with the children in this beautiful, peaceful place, I wondered if this was only a ruse to get my hopes up before I was taken back to confinement. I couldn't understand why I had been brought here.

An angelic figure enveloped in light and clothed in a bright white robe stood before me. "Your mother's prayers have reached the Queen of Heaven and God's throne. I am here to lead you to eternal life."

"Who are you?" I asked, refusing to move. "How do I know that this isn't another of Satan's tricks?"

"The Triune God doesn't permit him to cross the boundary to this holy place." Surely Satan and his followers would not use that expression; I wondered if this was my guardian angel. The angel smiled at me. "I have known you, Laura, from the very moment of your conception. Yes, I am your guardian angel."

"How should I address you? What is your name?"

"You may call me Yoel. It is a Hebrew word that means 'the Lord is God.' Where I dwell, ordinary human language is not needed. Yet, we are all partial to Aramaic and Hebrew because of the Lord, Jesus."

Upon reflection, the fact that my guardian angel had known me from the moment of my conception shook me to the core of my being. I recalled with shame how staunchly I had defended a woman's right to choose abortion, as well as human embryonic stem cell research and assisted suicide. My previous refusal to accept the truth that all human life is sacred and precious in the eyes of God and his angels now overwhelmed me with guilt and remorse.

My angel looked at me lovingly. "What do you want to say to God? He hears you even now."

I choked on my tears, crying out, "Lord, please forgive me!"

Yoel continued, "I have brought you to this place for a reason. You now understand that no unborn child is unloved or unwanted by God. This truth applies to the two children that you aborted."

I held my breath for a moment. For years, I had refused to think about my own abortions, and had almost managed to block them from my memory. Now I realized that, deep in my heart, I had always known that my babies were loved by God and that He was gravely offended by their destruction.

Without another word, Yoel gestured for me to follow him. I couldn't imagine what my angel was about to show me. He pointed to the merry-go-round in the distance. "There you will meet your children, Laura."

"No," I cried out, "Please don't do this to me. Don't punish me!"

Yoel responded gently, "This experience is not intended to punish you, Laura. It is meant to fully convert and heal you. It's not enough for you to accept that human life begins at conception and is sacred. It is not enough to regret your abortions. You must allow your heart to love your children and be loved by them."

My angel continued to walk ahead of me. "Will you come?"

"Yes!" I replied, tears streaming down my cheeks.

I wondered how my children would greet me, and if they had suffered when they were aborted. I quickened my pace, knowing that somehow my children would change me.

20

JAMES SIMONELLI, PH.D.

WITH A RENEWED sense of hope, James realized that Satan wasn't as powerful as he claimed to be; he couldn't read his thoughts nor compel him to speak. Satan was perceptive and carefully watched any reactions from his prey, and often correctly guessed at what people were thinking. James also realized that the beast's power must be fueled by unbelief and the malice of sin.

By reliving the beginning of his rebellion against God during his teenage years, James was forced to come to terms with his anger at Him. That anger had led him to fall deeper into mortal sin following the deaths of his baby brother and his mother.

Satan didn't know what had transpired after James left the antechamber. He didn't know that James had grown in self-knowledge by his visit to the past. When James came to appreciate the malice of his sins, a new spiritual path to rebirth had been forged in him. Also, while he was with the angel, James' physical wounds from the scourging and the fire had almost completely healed.

James looked around the darkened room. Appropriately, Satan stood in the midst of the dead ashes from the recent blaze; he had no life within and could only reign where everything was destroyed and lifeless. He thrived and reveled in the absence of God's grace.

"Where have you been, and what have you been doing, James?' demanded the beast. James remained silent, though he knew his refusal to answer might incur more punishment. "I command you to speak, James. What are you thinking?"

James stared at the creature. But instead of speaking to Satan, he raised his eyes to Heaven and cried out, "I declare before this unclean beast that I believe in one God, the Father almighty, maker of heaven and earth, of all things visible and invisible. I believe in one Lord Jesus Christ, the Only Begotten Son of God, born of the Father before all ages. God from God, Light from Light, true God from true God, begotten, not made, consubstantial with the Father; through him all things were made." At these words, James made the sign of the cross. Satan growled and retreated to the darkest corner of the room.

James continued his profession of faith, "For our sake he was crucified under Pontius Pilate, he suffered death and was buried, and rose again on the third day in accordance with the Scriptures. He ascended into heaven and is seated at the right hand of the Father. He will come again to judge the living and the dead and his kingdom will have no end. I believe in the Holy Spirit, the Lord, the giver of life, who proceeds from the Father and the Son, who with the Father and the Son is adored and glorified, who has spoken through the prophets."

With full conviction, James concluded the prayer, "I believe in one, holy catholic and apostolic Church. I confess one Baptism for the forgiveness of sins, and I look forward to the resurrection of the dead and the life of the world to come. Amen."

Satan roared like a lion and spewed flames out of his mouth from the corner of the room, but the flames were miraculously deflected from James' body. In the blink of an eye, James stood outside in a wooded area alive with colors and sweetly scented flowers. His mother, Martha, and his brother, Tommy, approached from the woods.

His mother looked just as she had before her death, only healthier and more joyful. Tommy, on the other hand, was no longer a two-year-old; he looked about seven.

"Mother? Is that you, Tommy? Am I in Heaven?"

Martha replied, "No, my precious son. You are still bound to the antechamber of Hell. Your trials are not yet over. Your brother and I have been permitted this visit before you die."

Then Martha put her hand on Tommy's shoulder. "You always wanted to see how he would look as a young child. Your wish has been granted by the Lord of Life."

Tommy smiled at his big brother, but spoke the words of an adult. "I know that my death was a grave blow to you. You were angry with God for taking me. You failed to see that whether we live or die, we belong to the Lord. I was never out of his loving sight for an instant."

"I still have trouble accepting the fact that a loving and merciful God would permit an innocent child to die of leukemia," James acknowledged. "I can't wrap my mind around that."

Tommy walked a few steps closer to his brother and looked into his troubled eyes. "It's not your mind that needs to wrap itself around God's will. He wants your heart to embrace his will!" Tommy paused and motioned for his brother to kneel beside him so they could speak face-to-face. "Death entered the world because of sin, not because of God! You foolishly rejected the truth about Original Sin. You tried to explain evil away by denying its existence. In God's original plan, disease, suffering and death were not to be part of human life. God created us to be immortal and to live in perfect love! Our Lord, the Incarnate Word, became flesh and blood to remedy the effects of the Original Sin and its consequences. Our Lord went so far as to allow himself to be crucified for our sins, and by the shedding of his own innocent blood we are healed and transformed. Sin and death lost their power when our Lord surrendered his life on the Cross for us. Like Christ, when I died, I became victorious! The Lord conquered death in me, and raised me to immortal and glorious life."

James continued to struggle with doubt. "Why would God permit Adam and Eve to sin? Why did God allow the whole human race to suffer for their sin?"

Ariel reappeared and hovered above them. "Listen with your heart to what I am about to teach you." James looked up at the angel. Without words, his guardian angel spoke to him about pure love. He concluded with audible words, "Pure love never coerces; it is freely given, freely invites, beckons and transforms the beloved. God, who is Love, did not coerce Adam and Eve to love him back. They chose rebellion, as did you, as all sinners do!"

James studied the faces of his mother and brother. "I have been such a fool all these years to deny God and hate him."

"Those who reject God's love and truth are fools," responded Tommy with a rueful glance at his brother.

"I always imagined that you would look just the way you do now," said James.

"Shortly after my death, I saw you looking at my baby photo," Tommy recalled. "You looked so angry. I begged the Lord then to allow me to visit you. But Jesus said that even if someone should rise from the dead, you would not believe in his love or goodness! Now that you are in the antechamber of Hell, it was the Lord himself who sent us to you. He loves you, James. He wants you with him forever."

James looked at his mother. "So I've been trapped in a spiritual dead-end for most of my life. I guess the only way out is love?"

Martha nodded, smiling approvingly. She led her son to a nearby pond, and together they peered down at the water.

Shortly, their reflection was replaced by the image of a woman standing on a snow-covered city rooftop.

"You proclaimed the Creed in the presence of the beast. I know that you believe what you just professed. But there is someone you poisoned with your atheistic teaching years ago. Because of your influence, she lost her faith and replaced it with drugs. Now she is an addict and has lost her job and her desire to live. Madison Drake is preparing to end her life. You must try to save her," Martha told him.

"I am sending you to Madison," Ariel confirmed. "She is about to leap to her death. She will hear you as though in a dream. Go to her!"

Tommy called, as the woods faded into nothingness, "We'll be waiting for you, James."

"We love you," his mother added.

21

DA'RELL THOMAS

DA'RELL BECAME CALMER as soon as he prayed for God's will and begged for help to accomplish it, even though he was still dangling over the bubbling cauldron. Closing his eyes and bracing himself to be scalded, he concentrated on remembering more of the words that Grandma Pearl had urged him to pray. "Lord Jesus, into your hands I commit my immortal soul," he said fervently. "Please, God, let me come to you."

Da'rell still expected to be lowered inch by inch into the pot. Instead, his chains disappeared and he felt a cool breeze on his face; he opened his eyes in amazement. He found himself standing in a lush garden.

He laughed with relief as he saw Grandma Pearl walk toward him, accompanied by a white-robed figure whose features were so brilliant that Da'rell could not look directly at them. Natural sunlight flooded the beautiful landscape, which was alive with greenery and wildflowers. Birds of all kinds and colors flew from one tree to another, filling the garden with their melodious chirping.

"Da'rell, you did good! The Lord heard your prayer. This time, your guardian angel is with me," Grandma Pearl said cheerfully. The angel bowed to Da'rell.

"So you're my guardian angel?" Da'rell inquired, squinting into the light.

"I have no name, but you may refer to me as Elior."

Grandma Pearl explained, "In Hebrew that means, 'My God is my light.'"

"This is correct. We use titles rather than names, even among ourselves," added Elior.

Turning, Grandma Pearl said, "I'll leave you with Elior. You'll be meeting our mother, Mary, very soon."

"Mary?"

"Elior has to enlighten you. Get it? My job here is done. I love you, Da'rell. Always have and always will!"

Grandma Pearl blew Da'rell a kiss as she disappeared. Then Da'rell turned to Elior, exclaiming, "I've read about angels in the Bible, but I never really thought I'd see one!"

"What you are about to see and experience is beyond words," replied his guardian.

Elior directed Da'rell's attention to another light shining from beyond a grove of trees. "The Queen is coming!" A white light positioned itself above a wild rose bush about ten yards from where they were standing. A dark-haired Jewish woman appeared. The angel bowed to the woman, and motioned for Da'rell to do the same.

The woman spoke in a gentle, soothing voice, "My dear child, I am Mary, the Immaculate Conception."

"I don't understand," Da'rell responded.

"Surrender your mind and heart to me, my son." Then the Blessed Mother communicated without words. Da'rell's soul began to understand her singular privilege of being conceived without Original Sin. He understood the Blessed Mother's fiat and her role in salvation history. He looked up at the Queen of Heaven and exclaimed, "O Mary, conceived without sin, pray for us who have recourse to you!"

The Blessed Mother smiled. "I am the Mother of Christ, the Mother of the Church, and the mother of all of humanity. Have no fear of death, Da'rell. My Son has conquered death and is the Lord of Life."

"Mother, must I go back to the antechamber? I no longer fear Satan. My only desire is to be carried in your arms to the throne of God."

"My dearest son, your contrition must be perfected. Then I will lift you up to be embraced by the Lord of Life."

The Blessed Mother continued silently. She impressed upon Da'rell that his guardian angel desired to speak to him before his passing from death to life, from imperfect contrition to perfect contrition.

While Elior communicated to Da'rell all that he needed to do to be saved, the Blessed Mother's image faded from the top of the wild rose. As she disappeared, she called out to Da'rell, "It is almost over. Take courage; He is calling you."

Elior taught his charge about the nature of all sin, and instructed him on how to attain perfect contrition. The angel communicated to Da'rell that perfect contrition would remit venial and mortal sins. He also explained that on earth, confession to a priest would normally be an important part of perfect contrition, for Catholics in particular. In Da'rell's case, his confession would be heard by Jesus Christ, the High Priest.

When the angel finished, Da'rell wiped away the tears streaming down his face. "It is so painful to think about my sins and how they offended God!"

"That is the beginning of perfect contrition," Elior explained. "Some people never regret their sins. They only regret the punishment due them."

His instructions complete, Elior slowly ascended to the heavens.

Without hesitation, Da'rell said, "I deserve the fires of Hell because of my sins."

Suddenly, he felt himself being drawn away from the beautiful wooded area. He knew what awaited him; he found himself suspended again above the boiling cauldron.

Satan reappeared in the room and began circling the cauldron.

"Were you out for a stroll, Da'rell? Oh, I know that your grandmother and that angel kidnapped you for a moment, but keep in mind that they have no control over your destiny. What did Elior say to you? Oh, I know your guardian angel! Are you surprised?" he asked, watching Da'rell's face. "I know all the angels! Your guardian and his kind chose to serve humanity. I, however, was created not to serve but to be served!"

Da'rell refused to reply.

"Your silence fascinates me," Satan said. "Don't you want to know what happened when I led the angelic rebellion against my enemy?"

Still, Da'rell made no response.

"Well, I'll tell you what happened, Da'rell. The Great One wanted me to bow in homage to the Word who was to become flesh and blood!"

It was evident from Satan's expression that referring to the Word of God caused him intense agony. "Can you imagine the absurdity of the Great One taking on human form—an inferior form? I promptly refused to worship such a creature! What was even more ludicrous was my enemy's insistence that we actually serve human beings—the likes of you—embodied spirits inferior to angelic beings. I rallied the other angels who refused to accept this plan. That was the beginning and the end of the rebellion. With one act of the will, I successfully led legions of angels to oppose the Great One's will. They now reign under me in my kingdom that will have no end! We shall never serve!" Satan emphasized proudly.

When Satan realized that Da'rell was again praying silently, he howled like a wild animal. "So be it. Boil! You're nothing but a worthless, filthy creature. As you boil, remember, you are mine for all eternity! I will have worse tortures in store for you!"

Although Da'rell knew that Satan would make all kinds of threats against him, he closed his eyes and prayed more fervently. Again and again, he cried out in his mind, "Lord Jesus, have pity on me, a poor sinner."

Da'rell felt the intense heat from the cauldron, but he refused to open his eyes or stop praying. He began to speak his prayer out loud. Over and over, he proclaimed his love for God and begged for mercy. Each time he cried out to the Lord, he became more aware of the malice of his sins and at the same time became more perfectly contrite for offending God.

Elior called out to Da'rell, "It is time. Your judgment begins."

Da'rell no longer hung above the cauldron of boiling water. When he opened his eyes, he was immersed in the brightest, blinding light. He knew that he was in the presence of Christ. In that instant, his entire life – all that he had ever said, desired or done – flashed before his eyes. The state of his soul throughout his earthly life was revealed. The condition of his soul at the instant of death was sealed. Da'rell died repentant and with perfect contrition. The voice of Christ declared, "Da'rell, you who desire life may come into my kingdom. First, be cleansed!"

With these final words, Da'rell entered the cleansing fires of Purgatory.

Da'rell found himself in a tiny, rustic cabin. He knew that the cabin was not a place, but rather a state of isolation to begin his purification.

The cabin was empty except for a lit candle in the middle of the floor. Glancing around, Da'rell saw that the shutters were sealed. He walked to the door, but it too was securely closed. "You may not go outside or anywhere else, Da'rell. You must dwell in solitude," said Elior's voice. There was absolutely nothing in the cabin to distract Da'rell from the candle. The cabin grew dark, and the candle became the center of his attention. The flame gave a warm light to the room, but much more importantly, it also enlightened Da'rell's soul.

Da'rell sat cross-legged on the wooden floor. Aloneness engulfed his soul. His agony had begun, but the flame consoled him. Elior spoke his final message to him, "Desire Him and you will be filled."

22

MADISON DRAKE

JAMES STOOD ON the roof of Madison Drake's apartment building. His former friend and student leaned over the ledge of the roof. She lifted a bottle of vodka to her mouth and took several gulps.

James called out to Madison. Intoxicated and wobbly on her feet, she turned and faced him. "How did you know I was here," she slurred. "I haven't seen you in years!"

Candidly, James replied, "I was sent by my angel to speak to you."

"An angel sent you to me? This must be some drug-induced hallucination," Madison replied sarcastically.

"You mustn't kill yourself," James said, as Madison raised her foot to mount the ledge.

Unnerved by the appearance of James and his message, Madison lowered her leg to the roof and shakily set the bottle of vodka on the ground. "Why are you here? What do you want from me?"

"This morning, I was riding on the N Train. A suicide bomber detonated a bomb in my compartment. I am between life and death, and have been sent to persuade you not to commit suicide."

Putting her hands on her hips, Madison laughed. "You've got to be kidding! Are you like an angel in disguise? I really suggest a different person next time." Looking up into the sky, she called out, "Excuse me! James is an atheist!"

"I'm no angel, Madison. I'm telling you the truth. A suicide bomber blew up my train. I am on the cusp of death, but I have been sent to persuade you to choose life."

"Why you?" asked Madison, mockingly.

"I led you away from God. I helped destroy your faith when you were a student at Princeton. I told you that God was nothing more than a myth. Remember? Eventually, you believed my lies."

"You flatter yourself too much, James. I didn't reject Christianity solely because of what you taught in your sociology class. But I'll admit that you got the ball rolling," Madison said. "You made me reconsider my religious beliefs. I came to my own conclusion that Christianity was a man-made religion. As a feminist, I searched for a belief system that conformed to my view of the world!"

Madison stopped talking and closed her eyes, momentarily absorbed in the drug-induced high that she had come to value more than life itself.

"Go on," James said. "You became a feminist."

Madison opened her brown eyes again and continued, "Christianity is a patriarchal religion. I searched the world's religions and discovered paganism. I'm not an atheist. I believe in a multiplicity of god-like forms, some of whom are feminine."

"Is paganism going to save you from Hell?" James asked her. "If you choose suicide, are your pagan gods going to save you from eternal damnation?"

"I don't believe in Hell or eternal damnation. It's all a myth!"

"I can assure you that Satan believes in you, Madison. He is lusting after your soul at this very moment," James told her.

Madison began to mumble, but James caught every word. "I believe we are all part of something bigger than ourselves. The Earth and nature are all expressions of the divine."

"It is the one, true God who created all things. He has no equal. Nature is part of his creation. Your attachment to paganism, in whatever form, is unreasonable and illogical. You once believed in Christ, Madison. He is the only one who can save you."

"I don't believe in Christ," Madison shouted, accidentally kicking the bottle of vodka over. In an attempt to save it, she bent over too quickly and became dizzy; she fell on her side and began to laugh.

James continued, "Christ's existence, mission and death are historical facts. His resurrection, of course, is ultimately a matter of faith. You once had faith in his resurrection. One day, you argued with me so persuasively that I questioned my own disbeliefs! How I wish I had listened to you. Now you listen to me. Please."

Madison looked at the bottle of vodka inches away from her on the ground. Its contents formed a puddle of clear liquid on the roof. "I must be really drunk," she laughed, then hiccupped.

"You chose the lethal combination of drugs and alcohol because you needed to numb your feelings in order to kill yourself. Look, Madison. Your angel is here," said James, pointing.

Startled by the appearance of a bright light, Madison cried out, "Who are you?"

"I am Eliana, which in Hebrew means 'my God has answered.' I am here to help you. You must not do what you are contemplating."

Madison sat up. "I must be going insane," she said, trying to focus her eyes on the angelic apparition.

"No. It is the sin within you that distorts, corrupts and perverts your thinking. To save your life, you must come to faith again," replied the angel.

James added, "I was wrong to convince you to leave the Catholic Church. Maybe you would have committed apostasy without my urging, but I still feel responsible for this final act of desperation."

"I have nothing to live for! I lost my job as a research scientist; Pivot Drugs fired me yesterday. I was at the top in my field! My career is over," cried Madison.

"You lost your job because of your addictions, but God wants you to live. You can always find another job. Your eternal destiny will only be determined once," Eliana stated firmly.

Madison closed her eyes tightly. "I am hallucinating..." She told herself that doing cocaine, popping pills and drinking vodka had taken its toll on her mind. She stumbled to her feet and turned again to the ledge. She leaned up against it, looking back at James and her angel as they prayed.

"Go away! Leave me alone!" she cried.

Off in the distance was a beautiful, elegant creature who also appeared to be an angel. "That's right, Madison. Order them to go away! I'll only speak to you alone," the being insisted. "I am one of the goddesses you have worshipped. Order them to leave!"

James interrupted the creature's words. "Even demons may appear as angels of light! As a pagan, you worshipped demons— fallen angels. They dwell in Hell and want you to join their misery. This angel hates you and only wants to destroy you. Ask this demon whether or not it wishes to serve the Triune God, if you doubt the truth of my words."

Madison was confused. Did she believe in the one, true God, or did she believe in multiple gods and goddesses as a follower of Wicca? Did she believe in fallen angels?

"You're right, Madison. You should jump from the ledge. Once you are liberated from your feeble body, you can be at peace. Don't be afraid. Do it!" said the demon in disguise.

Madison stared at the beautiful, angelic creature. "Answer the question. Do you wish to serve the Triune God?"

The creature glared at her with hatred. "I won't respond to such a silly question."

Eliana pleaded with Madison. "I am your guardian angel. To jump is to plunge into Hell. Ask the other spirit its name."

"What's your name?" demanded Madison, "Tell me at once!"

The spirit howled, "My name is רוציה לפש."

"I don't understand what that means," replied Madison.

Eliana explained, "It means 'vile creature.' That is the demon's title, if you will."

Madison stared at the beautiful, angelic figure; it was transformed into a hideous demon as she watched.

Frightened, Madison turned to Eliana and pleaded, "Make it go away!"

"Depart to the depths of Hell where you belong," ordered Eliana.

"I believe in God," yelled Madison, "I do believe!"

Eliana ordered Madison to leave the roof at once. "When you are sober, you must turn your life around and give it back to God. Do you understand?" Madison nodded. James felt himself pulled away from the scene; he was unable to utter another word.

Meanwhile, Madison was left alone on the roof. She stumbled to the door and down a flight of stairs to the elevators. She wondered if what had just transpired really was only a figment of her imagination or a drug-induced hallucination. Then a man, a very handsome man in an elegant tuxedo, stopped at the elevator to offer his assistance.

"Are you ill," asked the man, sympathetically, "May I help you to your apartment?"

Madison stared. "Do I know you?"

As Satan extended his hand toward hers, a voice from within Madison whispered, "Beware."

Madison snatched her hand away. "I don't need any help," she replied, though her slurred speech seemed to contradict her words. "I'm fine."

"I was only trying to be a good neighbor," replied Satan with a hint of sarcasm. "Maybe we'll meet again real soon."

Suddenly dizzy, Madison leaned against the wall. "Leave me alone!" she told the stranger.

"So be it," Satan replied, making no attempt to hide his annoyance. Just then the elevator doors opened; Madison stepped inside and pressed the button for the sixth floor. Satan glared as the doors closed between them.

Seconds later, Madison arrived on her floor and fumbled clumsily in the pocket of her jeans for the key to her apartment. Once inside, she bolted the door and collapsed on the luxurious leather couch in the living room. Immediately, she fell into a deep sleep. In a dream, she remembered Eliana, James, and the demon that had appeared to her on the roof. She also remembered the handsome man in the tuxedo who made her feel so uneasy as she waited for the elevator.

Madison awoke several times, saying aloud each time, "No more dreams. I believe."

Later that evening, the effects of the drugs and alcohol in her system had diminished significantly. As she sat on the edge of the couch, Madison began to have serious doubts that she had ever gone to the roof to commit suicide. She opened the liquor cabinet; the bottle of vodka was missing. Eventually, her doubts about the intended suicide evaporated when she realized that she still had her winter parka on. Her jeans and running shoes were still damp from the snow.

Madison removed her jacket and stared in the mirror at her disheveled blond hair and at the mascara smudges around her eyes. Although she was only twenty-nine, she looked at least ten years older.

It was time to give some serious thought to the direction her life should take. Without her high-paying job, she would have to sell her luxury condo. Despite losing her job, despite the other hardships she faced – including drug rehabilitation – she was relieved that she hadn't ended her life. She knew that she was meant to live a productive life, not a self-destructive one.

She returned to the living room, picked up the remote control for the television, and entered the channel for the local news broadcast. She needed to hear human voices and to connect with the world again.

The newscaster reported that thirty-two passengers had perished on the N Train from Brooklyn to Manhattan that morning, when a terrorist had committed suicide by detonating explosives. In addition, at least ten people were in serious condition, and many others had been treated for minor injuries.

Madison recalled that James had told her that he was one of the victims on the N Train that morning. "James, I really did see you on the roof! It wasn't all a dream," Madison said aloud. At that moment, she made a firm decision to reform her life. She had been given a second chance. She had lost her job, but not her life, and she was intent on not losing her soul. Madison wanted and needed to change her life for the better by returning to her faith and beginning treatment for her addictions. This could not be accomplished on her own; she would need medical help within hours if she was to begin a life of sobriety.

An Internet search using the words, "drug and alcohol rehabilitation facilities in New York" revealed numerous locations where an addict could receive help. Before she had time to change her mind, Madison used the voice command on her cell phone to reach her widowed mother. Weeping, she poured out her heart and meekly asked for her mother's help.

"Thank God!" was her mother's heartfelt reply, before arranging to pick Madison up within the hour.

23

DA'RELL THOMAS

DESPITE NO LONGER living in time, it seemed to Da'rell that he had been staring at the flame of the candle for days, weeks or months. In addition to the lit candle, he had been given a crucifix shortly after his arrival at the cabin. The corpus of Christ was exquisitely carved from ebony. He held the crucifix in his hands, then brought it to his lips and kissed it repeatedly during the most difficult moments of his purification.

As Da'rell stared into the flame, all his sins, every act of rebellion against God that he had ever committed, became clear to him. He grieved for every time he had offended the Lord. When he could grieve and cry no more, he sat in silent and loving adoration, knowing that hidden beyond the flame was the Lord of Light. His intense desire for the Lord gave him the greatest agony.

Then, out of the silence, Da'rell heard Elior's voice, "It is time."

Da'rell rose from the floor, and following his angel, passed through the closed cabin door. Together they made their way down to the lake that was just outside the cabin. He was surprised to see a man wearing a white tunic standing in a boat offshore. He immediately recognized the man as Saint Peter.

Saint Peter called out to Da'rell to join him. Da'rell walked in the lake up to his ankles, but the saint gestured for him to stop. "No. It is time for you to walk on the water."

Da'rell lifted his right foot and then his left, and stood on the water. He walked to the little boat and stepped into it; there he received a hearty welcome from the former fisherman of Galilee. "As you cross with me to the other shore, you will understand all that you need to know about our Lord and the Church he established for the salvation of the world."

At Peter's invitation, Da'rell sat down across from him in the boat. The two men conversed wordlessly as they sailed to the other shore. As Saint Peter revealed the truth of the Gospels to him, Da'rell felt that he had actually been with the Twelve while Jesus completed His mission on Earth. He was filled with wonder and delight as he relived their experiences with the Master.

The small boat moved made its way to the final destination. Saint Peter stood up, inviting Da'rell to do the same. He pointed to the sky above. "Our beloved Queen awaits you." Da'rell understood that Peter was referring to Mary, the mother of Christ.

A woman appeared in the sky, bathed in a rainbow of lights; a crown of twelve stars encircled her head. "Come to me, my child," beckoned the Blessed Virgin, with outstretched arms.

Saint Peter nodded his head, "Go to her."

Da'rell closed his eyes and held out his arms to Mary. Within his soul he whispered, "Take me home, Mother most pure."

24

James Simonelli, Ph.D

James' mission with Madison complete, the apartment building and everything else in sight, including Ariel, faded away.

"The time has come for your judgment. You have passed over from life to death, from time to eternity. Prepare your soul."

At once, James was blinded by an intense white light. Then he heard a voice—the voice of Christ calling his name, and instructing him to walk into the light of truth. He did as he was commanded, and opened his eyes to see the image of Christ Pantocrator, ruler of all.

James could not see Ariel, but heard his voice, "Your particular judgment begins. Either the truth will set you free for eternal life in Heaven or the truth will condemn you to Hell."

At that instant, James' entire life flashed before his eyes. All that he had ever thought, said and done became clear, and the state of his soul was made manifest. James cried out with joy that he had died repentant and with perfect contrition, and he heard the voice of the Lord declare, "James, you who desire life may come into my Kingdom. First, be cleansed!" With these final words, James entered the cleansing fires of Purgatory.

James found himself alone in a small tent. He understood that his time on earth was over, that at this moment his body had ceased to live. He knew that his time in the tent would cleanse his soul from all the stains of sin and its effects, but he did not yet realize that Purgatory would be both terribly painful and delightful at the same time.

The inside of the tent was bare except for a large crucifix suspended in the air. The realistic image of the crucified Christ took James by surprise. He knelt before the crucifix and kissed the feet of Christ. Then he backed away from the cross and opened the flap of the tent, but found that he was unable to go past the entrance. Clearly, he would spend his Purgatory alone within the tent.

The tent stood in a barren desert, but in the distance James could see a lush oasis. However, he knew that his spirit must be completely purged before his journey to the oasis. James turned back to the crucifix and knelt down to pray.

Although he could not see Ariel, he heard the angel's voice. "Your sins will be burned away in the heat of the Lord's charity, and in solitude."

James wrapped both arms around the bottom of the cross for what seemed like hours, days or even months. Finally, he stood up and reached for the nailed feet of Christ. Expecting to feel only wood, he was amazed to find blood flowing from the crucified feet of the image. Time seemed to stand still again; James had no idea how long he kissed the feet of the Lord and wept for his sins. He only knew that he longed to be with Christ, whose image was now his only consolation.

25

CATHY PETERSEN

CATHY, STILL HOLDING Angelica in the empty lobby of the abortion clinic, glowed with joy at finally meeting her daughter and receiving her forgiveness. After a few moments, Angelica broke away from Cathy's hug and said excitedly, "Wait here. I have a surprise for you. I'll be right back. Close your eyes!"

As difficult as it was for Cathy to let Angelica out of her sight, she reluctantly closed her eyes. "You can look now," Angelica sang out a few seconds later. In the child's hand was a single red rose. "Take it, Mommy. It smells good." As Cathy clutched the rose in her hand, the little girl continued, "Be careful of the thorns. I know you love roses. The other day, when you went to the flower shop, you looked at a rose just like this one, and thought of me."

Cathy nodded, "Yes, I went to the florist to purchase a bouquet of flowers for a co-worker who was in the hospital. She had just delivered a baby girl. I found it hard to rejoice about my friend's baby because I remembered the day that I destroyed you. I wondered about you, but I'm confused. You died in my womb. How is it that you are appearing to me as a little girl?"

"My appearance is for your sake. I don't want you to fear me. I want you to love me, so that I can help you. I want to be with you forever in Heaven." Angelica snuggled closer as Cathy breathed in the rose's fragrance. "I know you regret the abortion that took my physical life." She grabbed her mother's hand and tugged her toward the exit, but before they reached it, the lobby faded away and they found themselves in an open field. There, other little children were running and playing with angels whom Cathy assumed must be their guardians.

This place was familiar; it was very similar to the field Cathy had encountered after escaping the room filled with decaying corpses. Again, she heard the music of a merry-go-round playing in the background. This time, she followed Angelica as she ran with the other children and their angels to mount the ponies.

Angelica squeezed her mother's hand and gestured for her to kneel down beside her. She whispered, "These children were unwanted, too. A few of them were destroyed only moments ago at Innovation Health Care Options. Their guardian angels rescued them and brought them here to help them discover who they are, and to prepare them to meet the Lord."

"Angelica, why did you bring me here?"

"To learn, repent and love," the child said, gazing into her mother's eyes.

"Do you know about your father?" Cathy asked.

"My angel told me that he is married to another woman and has other children. He didn't want me. I know that you wanted me, but you were too weak."

"I was a fool, Angelica! I should never have chosen Jason over you!"

"You can't undo the choice you made to abort me. What you can do is make life-giving choices right now. This is what God wills," Angelica said emphatically.

Cathy's attention was diverted from the children on the merry-go-round as she pondered her daughter's words. Angelica yanked on her mother's hand. "Hurry, the children are getting ready for the ride! I already know who I am, but I will take this ride so you can learn who I am." The children lined up, and Angelica dropped her mother's hand so she could join them. Giggling, she climbed aboard a golden pony under a jeweled dome.

The smallest children were placed on the ponies by their guardian angels, who floated back to the ground once their wards were seated. The music started, and the children laughed and shouted with delight as their golden ponies turned into real white ponies.

As the ponies circled the carousel, the children learned the truth about their short lives. Their initial shouts of joy came to an abrupt end when they saw images of their parents and family members, and they understood their plight in life. All of the children cried as they realized that they had been unwanted. Then they were bathed in a soft white light—God's healing light. Their sobs ceased when they realized that they were always wanted and loved by their God. They rejoiced when they learned that the Son of God had died for them and yearned for them to join Him in his Eternal Kingdom.

At the realization that they were loved beyond all measure, the children found peace and profound joy. Some of them cried out, "Praise to God the Father, God the Son and God the Holy Spirit."

As the ponies continued to gallop around the immense carousel, Angelica passed Cathy several times. Each time, she waved and blew kisses to her. Each time, Cathy discovered something new about her daughter, from her favorite color to her favorite fairy tale. Angelica and the other children grew and matured in appearance as they rode; the ponies grew larger as well. When the music stopped, they were no longer children riding on ponies, but young adults seated on white horses. One by one, they dismounted and walked solemnly back to their angels, who welcomed them with a hug.

Afterwards, some of the angels introduced their charges to other deceased family members who had already reached the Heavenly Kingdom. New loving and everlasting relationships were immediately established.

Uzziel came and stood next to Cathy. He pointed to a young Chinese woman who had been joined by several other young women. "In China, they have a one-child policy. This girl was aborted only minutes ago. Her sisters were waiting for her."

Cathy watched as the young women, all very excited to meet each other, embraced and spoke in Mandarin. Uzziel then directed Cathy's attention to her own daughter as she walked toward her with her guardian angel.

Angelica came and stood beside Cathy. She looked so much like Jason. The resemblance stunned Cathy, and at the same time made her heart ache.

"Mother, I've journeyed on this carousel many times. I always stop at this point, as a young woman. Of course, this age reflects what I would have looked like in time. I still have much to learn about the Creator and about myself. Very soon, my self-knowledge and love of God will allow me to journey beyond this temporary state to the Eternal Kingdom."

"So, all this time, you've been trying to find out who you are?"

"No. My spiritual journey is to discover who God wants me to be. When you aborted me, my guardian angel gathered me up in his arms and brought me into the presence of the Lord. I couldn't see Him yet or comprehend in whose presence I dwelled. I suppose I was like a newborn in the arms of her mother. I only knew that I was safe. Whenever my soul cried out to God, he embraced me and made me understand that I am loved. Since I never had the opportunity on Earth to re-spond properly to God's invitation to love, I now experience his love and my love for him in countless mysterious ways!"

"It's so hard for me to grasp all of this."

"Mystery is always difficult to grasp. Follow me to the pool of images," Angelica replied.

They arrived at a beautiful pool of clear, clean water. "See now what your choice meant for me and many others." Cathy looked into the water and saw the reflection of a large group of people posed as if for a portrait. "There I am," stated Angelica, "Watch and learn." She pointed to the boy she would have married, "He was aborted as well, by his mother." Next she identified the children that she would have borne, and their descendants. "Your great-great-great-grandson would have found a cure for most forms of cancer."

Cathy stared at the young man. He reminded her of her father as a young adult.

"What have I done?" Cathy groaned. "If they were never conceived, where are they?"

Angelica smiled, "For God, all things are possible. They remain in his eternal and loving heart."

"I don't understand," said Cathy.

"How can you understand? It is beyond our ability to think or to love as our mysterious God loves!"

"I am so sorry for what I've done! If only I could undo it!"

"I told you that we can never undo the past. We can alter the present, which in turn affects the future. My desire is that in the present moment you choose life." Angelica began to back away. "Mother, I have to leave you."

"Don't leave me! I never want to lose you again!"

Angelica returned to Cathy's side and put her arms around her. "I love you; I will be waiting for you on the other side. It's up to you to desire eternal life with God."

Cathy clung tightly to her daughter. "Forgive me, Angelica. Forgive me for being so selfish."

Angelica smiled gently, "You are forgiven and loved by me for all eternity," then disappeared.

"My baby, my baby," Cathy cried over and over again, feeling just as empty as she had the day after her abortion.

Uzziel reappeared and approached Cathy. "It is time for

you to return to the antechamber of Hell. I can hold you back no longer. Do what you must to choose life."

"No! Please, not the antechamber ..."

Before she could finish the sentence, Cathy found herself back in the room filled with decaying corpses. This time, she stood her ground and refused to retreat. One of the corpses reached out and grabbed her arm. Within her spirit, Uzziel instructed her to pray. She could hear her angel's voice clearly as he spoke in the depths of her being, and she was no longer terrified. Uzziel had been speaking to her all the time that she was in the antechamber, but her fear had silenced his voice in her soul.

Satan appeared in front of Cathy as she prayed. His rage was beyond words. "Blasphemy," he screamed, "Tear her apart!"

Uzziel had taught Cathy how to make the sign of the cross in praise of the Holy Trinity. She did so now, and Satan vanished like a puff of smoke. The corpses backed away as her guardian angel once more became visible.

Satan reappeared, but cowered in the presence of the angel. "You have no right! I'm the Master here. My subjects do as I command! She's mine!"

Uzziel told Cathy, "Do what you have been instructed to do."

Cathy nodded as the angel left her side to hover above the room. She faced her accuser, the beast and the Father of Lies. "I am guilty of terrible sins, and have offended the Almighty Lord." She reached into her pocket and pulled out the receipt for her abortion. "Among my many sins was the destruction of my baby, Angelica. My child has forgiven me and now I beg the Lord of life to forgive me!"

Cathy ripped the paper in half and tossed the pieces into the air. Satan made a grab for the fragments, but growled as Uzziel retrieved them and they disappeared at his touch. "Forgiveness is not that easy," Satan snarled.

"God's forgiveness is pure and simple," Cathy rejoined. She again signed herself with the cross and continued, "I reject you, all your works and all your empty promises, with every ounce of my being. You are the Father of Lies, and you try to destroy anyone in your path. You whispered to my soul that my life with Jason was worth more than the loss of my child. You told me that his love for me was worth more than an unwanted pregnancy. You told me I had a right to be happy even if that meant having an affair with a married man. You are a liar!"

Cathy cried out, "In the name of the Lord Jesus, I beg forgiveness for my sins and the salvation of my soul!"

Satan growled and hissed, "No! No! You're mine! I'll never let you go!"

At that very instant, Cathy left the antechamber of Hell and found herself enveloped in intensely white, blinding light. She heard a voice, the voice of Christ, calling out her name. "I am the Good Shepherd who goes in search of his lost sheep." The Lord then instructed her to walk deeper into the light so that she might see. Cathy did as she was commanded and opened her eyes to see Christ standing before her in glory. Without hesitation, she praised Him, "My Lord and my God!"

Cathy could not see Uzziel, but heard his voice. "Your particular judgment begins. The truth will either set you free for eternal life in Heaven or will condemn you to Hell."

Looking up, Cathy saw only the light of Christ. Without spoken words, her entire life was represented in images. At her particular judgment, the Lord spoke to her heart and she fully understood all of the thoughts, desires and actions of her life. Finally, an audible voice declared, "Cathy, you who desire life, come into my Kingdom. First, be cleansed!"

As she heard these words, she entered into Purgatory, which for her consisted of confinement in a sandstone sea cave. She could smell the salt water and see the waves on the coast, but she was unable to leave the cave and walk out onto the beach.

The ceiling of the cave was so low that Cathy had to hunch over to make her way to the far end, where a small fire burned on a low rocky shelf. The beach outside slowly grew dark until the only light came from the fire; Cathy knelt down beside it. She could still hear the crash of the ocean, but she could see nothing other than the flames of truth and love that danced before her eyes. Cathy had never felt more alone, but Uzziel's final message was one of consolation and hope, "Desire him and you will be filled."

26

JAMES SIMONELLI, PH.D.

IT WAS IMPOSSIBLE for James to know whether he was in the tent for hours, years, or even decades as time was measured on earth, but finally, he heard Ariel's voice, "It is time to cross the desert."

James heeded the voice of his angel and backed away from the Cross. He kept his eyes fixed on the feet of the crucified Lord, still feeling unworthy to look upon the face of the Lord, even in an image. At the entrance of the tent, he genuflected toward the crucifix and emerged into the blinding light of the desert sun. As James remembered his sins, faults and failings, pain surged throughout his body. The soles of his feet burned on the hot sand, which James recognized as symbolic of the effects in his soul of the mortal sins he had committed throughout his life.

James walked slowly and deliberately toward the oasis, despite the intense heat. The lushness of the green plants and trees in the distance soothed his soul. Though the oasis seemed far away at first, James covered the distance very quickly and was soon enjoying the cool ground on his feet beneath the shade of a tree. After a brief rest, he made his way over to a stone well that stood in the middle of the oasis. He leaned over the edge and thirsted for the clear water that was just beyond his reach. As he looked up again, he spotted an old Mexican-Indian approaching. The man carried a wooden pail and a long rope.

When he was close enough for conversation, James asked, "Who are you? Are you being purged as well?"

Tying the rope onto the bucket, the Indian laughed, "No, Señor James. I was sent from Heaven to bring you relief." He threw the bucket down into the well. As he did so, James smiled, realizing that – like everything else he encountered now – the wood from the bucket made him think of the wood of the cross. The bucket hit the water with a splash; while waiting for it to fill up, the Indian exclaimed, "This water gives life!" He hauled it up and removed a golden cup that hung on his belt. The man filled it with water and told him, "Drink and be refreshed, my friend."

James dipped the golden chalice into the water again and again, and drank until his intense thirst was satisfied. He turned to his companion and asked, "Are you an angel?"

The old Indian shook his head, "No. I'm not an angel. I am one of the saints in Heaven. You may call me Juanito. That's the name the Blessed Mother used when she spoke to me on Earth. She appeared to me, a poor, ignorant man, to tell my people and all the people of the world that she is our Heavenly Mother."

James pointed a finger at the stranger. "You must be Juan Diego! It was Our Lady of Guadalupe who appeared to you. She led millions of your people in Mexico to convert in the sixteenth century."

"Yes. With their conversions to Christ and the Church, they stopped sacrificing their children to false gods—to the demons," added Juan Diego. "The Evil One was enraged."

"Your tilma still hangs in the basilica in Mexico City."

"As a college professor, you traveled to Mexico City," Juan Diego said. "You entered the basilica and stood before Our Lady's miraculous image on the tilma, and you laughed. I know. I saw you!"

James nodded, deeply ashamed of his blasphemous behavior. "Now I understand," he apologized. "Why am I here, in this oasis?"

"Purgatory is a very fertile place, but you could only appreciate it in the desert of your soul. Here, you have finally come to knowledge, truth and purity. The oasis is temporary, as is Purgatory. Soon you will see God face-to-face. The oasis is a symbol of life that emerges from the experience of the desert. From the burning desert you will be delivered to the fullness of life," explained St. Juan Diego.

James looked up as he heard the rustling sound of a breeze through the palm trees. A sweet smell of roses permeated the area. "She is coming, James," Juan said, bowing his head. Transparent beings from all the choirs of angels filled the oasis: Seraphim, Cherubim, Thrones, Dominations, Virtues, Powers, Principalities, Archangels and Angels. All of them demonstrated profound respect and love for the Blessed Mother as she appeared.

Ariel, too, appeared and shouted, "Behold the Woman!"

Our Lady of Guadalupe appeared now, looking as she had when she appeared to Juan Diego. Her garments sparkled in the sunlight, which formed an arc behind her. Her long dark hair glistened in the sunlight, as well. Although he had no knowledge of the Indian dialect that she spoke, James understood every word spoken to him by Mary. "Come into my arms, my son."

As a young child raises his arms to be picked up by his mother, James raised his arms and cried out, "Mother, please take me home!"

27

CATHY PETERSEN

CATHY STARED INTO the fire as she sat on the floor of the sandstone cave, almost consumed by loneliness. Uzziel appeared next to her and handed her a crucifix. "Behold your Lord on the Cross. Contemplate his love for you."

Before Cathy could respond, the angel left her. She clutched the crucifix in her hands and brought it to her chest, finding immediate relief in her soul. Cathy had no idea how long she had been praying in earthy time, but it seemed like forever.

In her purgative state, she learned the truth about Christ, his Church and its saving mission in the world. Her heart ached for those who did not know the Savior of the world or his unconditional love for them.

When her own heart was completely cleansed from the effects of sin, Uzziel reappeared and said, "It is time to approach the ocean of mercy."

Without further instruction, Cathy arose. She and Uzziel walked out of the cave toward the ocean, a magnificent sight. She knew that beyond it and through it the Lord awaited her.

As she and her angel walked together across the sand, a religious sister dressed in a black habit approached them on the beach. Cathy was instantly infused with knowledge about Saint

Faustina, the Apostle of Divine Mercy. It was to this Polish nun that the Lord had appeared in visions with a message of mercy for the entire world—a world that would soon be immersed in World War II.

Cathy listened as Saint Faustina spoke to her, "In my visions, the Lord taught me that the greatest sinners should place their trust in His mercy. They had the right before others to trust in the abyss of His mercy. The Lord said that He was delighted by souls who make an appeal to His mercy. To such souls he would grant even more graces than they requested. He said that he would not punish even the greatest sinner if that person made an appeal to His compassion. Before he would come as judge to the world, he would first open the door of His unfathomable and inscrutable mercy. You, Cathy, have been immersed in the Lord's Divine Mercy."

Cathy responded, "His justice would certainly have condemned me to eternal punishment for my many sins. I know now that only his mercy has spared me!"

Faustina nodded. "His love and mercy are boundless! God's mercy was extended to you in a very special way before your death. While you were about to die in the explosion, a pious woman recited the Chaplet of Divine Mercy. She offered her prayers for a soul in danger of losing salvation. You were that soul! Your initial conversion, when you remembered the Good Shepherd in the Lucifer Stadium, coincided with her prayers."

To Cathy's amazement, the ocean became still and she heard a multitude of angels praising Christ, "Holy, Holy, Holy, Lord God of hosts. Heaven and Earth are full of your glory and loving mercy." Cathy understood that the angels were announcing the Lord of Life, and she squinted at the bright light that still hid him from her sight. Beside the blinding light stood a woman dressed in blue with a crown of precious gems. She knew that this was Mary, the Mother of God. The Blessed Mother hovered over the ocean of mercy with the brilliant light at her back. With a gentle breeze, she glided closer to the shore where Cathy, Faustina and Uzziel stood. Our Lady introduced herself, "I am Mary, Mother of Divine Mercy. Come, my child, and be with my Son forever. He longs for you."

Saint Faustina led Cathy into the ocean of mercy that swirled around her feet. Cathy looked up, crying, "Mother, bring me to the fount of Mercy!"

28

The Father of Lies

S ATAN GROWLED CURSES as Da'rell, James and Cathy transcended the antechamber of Hell. He knew that they had been purged and glorified, and he moaned miserably in defeat. His pride burned within him; he had to admit his enemy had triumphed.

To boost his wounded ego, he called to mind his decision that he would never serve God. As he fed his pride with memories of his rebellion, he effortlessly quoted the Scripture passages that accused him. The first passage that made him curse God came from the Book of Revelation. He recalled the words:

"There was war in heaven. Michael and his angels fought against the dragon, and the dragon and his angels fought back. But he was not strong enough, and they lost their place in heaven. The great dragon was hurled down—that ancient serpent called the devil, or Satan, who deceives the whole world. He was hurled to the earth, and his angels with him.[**Revelation 12:7-9**]"

A passage from the Book of Isaiah enraged him further:

"How you have fallen from heaven, O Lucifer, son of the dawn!

You have been cast down to the earth, you who once laid low the nations!

You said in your heart, 'I will ascend to heaven; I will raise my throne above the stars of God;

I will sit enthroned on the mount of assembly, on the utmost heights of the sacred mountain.

I will make myself like the Most High.' But you are brought down to the grave, to the depths of the pit."

[Isaiah 14:12-15]

Satan's fury at his own miserable fate made him even more determined to make sure that Laura O'Malley would never leave his kingdom. He smiled, noting that her moment of crossing from life to death was about to occur.

29

LAURA O'MALLEY

YOEL STOOD BESIDE me as the merry-go-round started to turn. The lively music and the children's laughter made me even more curious to discover the two children that I had aborted.

My first abortion had occurred six years earlier. When I informed my live-in boyfriend, John, that I was pregnant, he made it clear that he wasn't ready to be a father or even to consider marriage. After the abortion, I plunged into a deep depression. Despite my medical background, I ignored the fact that my mental condition was a result of the procedure; I attributed my emotional state to hormone imbalance. Even when I suffered from recurrent nightmares about a lost child crying for help, I couldn't admit to myself that the abortion was such an assault against life that it wreaked havoc in my body and soul.

Still, I decided to have a second abortion when my relationship with John ended. I found out I was pregnant the week he left our apartment, and he never even knew about the pregnancy. At that point, we were barely even on speaking terms. I arranged for the abortion and told myself that bringing an unwanted child into the world would be selfish. Once again, I became depressed, and I began to detest myself as well as John.

All this was on my mind as I strained to see the faces of the children passing by on the merry-go-round. I had always imagined that I had aborted a boy first and then a girl. My belief was confirmed when my guardian angel pointed at my two children, both preschool age, riding side-by-side. I began to weep.

"Watch," commanded Yoel.

With each turn of the merry-go-round, my son and daughter grew older; now they looked like teenagers. When the ride came to an end, they appeared to be young adults.

I couldn't take my eyes off them; they both resembled me in some ways, yet they were both unique individuals. My son looked strong and serious, but his twinkling eyes revealed a young man who would laugh easily. The young lady beside him was blue-eyed, with my strawberry-blonde curls. Tears flowed down my cheeks as my children approached. My son, a full head taller than me, bent down to dry my cheeks. "Our angels said that you should name us."

My daughter took hold of my hands. "It's all right."

A lump had formed in my throat. I swallowed and said, "Why should I name you? I don't deserve such an honor!"

"We know how much you regret what you did," my daughter replied. "You told yourself that we weren't fully human, but you knew that wasn't true. You cried on the anniversaries of our abortions. You kept that secret from everyone, but God saw you cry and so did we. We forgive you. Please name us."

I had never felt such love. "It was my sin that kept you from glorifying God with your lives. As God is my judge, I admit my sin and beg for his mercy. As for your names, well…" I turned to my angel for assistance. Yoel nodded and said, "In Hebrew, the name Daniel means, 'God is my judge.'"

I looked at my son first, declaring, "Your name is Daniel." Then to my daughter, "Your name is Danielle." They put their arms around me, and Daniel said quietly, "I was the first baby that you aborted. When Danielle died, I greeted her first, even before her angel. We are as close as siblings can be!"

Danielle whispered in my ear, "He's the best brother this side of eternity!" What a joy it was to share a joke with my children; I laughed and cried at the same time. The knowledge that my children loved me both pierced my soul and healed it.

Yoel interrupted our conversation, "Laura, it is time. You have passed from life to death, from time to eternity. Your judgment begins."

No longer in the presence of my children, I now found myself immersed in the brightest, blinding light. I felt Christ's presence, and knew that He was hidden in the light. My entire life flashed before me. The choices and events in my life that had alienated me from God were represented in rapidly flashing images. With each image, I knew what I was thinking, feeling and willing at all times and all at once. I was fully aware of every sin that I had ever deliberately committed. The state of my soul was made clear. I also knew that the condition of my soul at the instant of death was permanently sealed. I was grateful for my encounter with my children; it had brought me to complete conversion, repentance and perfect contrition.

The voice of the Lord declared, "Laura, you who desire life may come into my Kingdom. First, be cleansed!" With these final words, I immediately entered the cleansing fires of Purgatory.

I found myself on top of a high mountain. I walked to a precipice and peered over the edge. Looking up, I saw clouds in the sky; looking down, I saw only a cloudy mist.

A short distance from the precipice, a small campfire was burning. The daylight began to diminish until the mountain was in total darkness except for the campfire. I longed for shelter, but knew that my Purgatory had to leave me cold, exposed and vulnerable.

I could see only a few feet beyond the fire. I knelt down and discovered a crucifix about three feet long on the ground. The corpus was made of carved ivory. Embracing the crucifix, I stared into the fire.

Intense aloneness engulfed my soul so completely that I could only cry out for mercy. I heard Yoel's voice, "Desire him and you will be filled."

30

Laura O'Malley

You may wonder how long I stared at the fire as I prayed on the mountain. Since Purgatory is beyond time, the experience of purgation is timeless. However, once I had been purged, the most profound peace enveloped my soul.

You must understand that my descriptions of the Antechamber of Hell and of Purgatory have been imbedded with symbolic images that convey profound spiritual realities.

One insight that Cathy, James, Da'rell, and I wanted to share with you about Purgatory is that the suffering endured, in this temporary spiritual state, is caused primarily from the yearning for total union with God. That yearning serves as a catalyst that burns away all the dross from souls. With no imperfections to impede union with God, Purgatory ends as the soul ascends to God's infinite love.

When my purgation ended, Yoel summoned me one last time. I expected to meet the Queen of Heaven before entering the everlasting presence of God, but eternity is full of surprises. Yoel smiled and said, "They are waiting for you."

I floated to the mountain precipice and hovered in mid-air. There, surrounded by brilliant light, appeared my beloved Daniel and Danielle. They held out their arms to me and cried out, "Mother, let us go home."

I lifted my arms to my children and was swept into their loving embrace.

With the Blessed Mother and the multitude of angels and saints, my children and I were received into the presence of the Triune God. Our love was consummated in glory.

* * *

I have been permitted to speak a few words about Ahmed, the suicide bomber on the N Train who was responsible for the act of terrorism that took so many lives. I can tell you that he is not among the living in Heaven. Is he in Hell, or in Purgatory? This is not for me to reveal.

What is certain is that Ahmed's fate rests with the God of Creation—the One True and Eternal God. The truth is that that there is only one way to Heaven, and that is through the Lord of Life. The boundless mercy of our Lord and Savior, Jesus Christ, the Word made flesh and blood, makes salvation possible for all people, even the suicide bomber known as Ahmed.

Ahmed's eternal fate will be revealed definitively at the Final Judgment. His final thoughts and desires will be made known to all.

On what shall Ahmed and every human person be judged at the moment of death? "We are all judged on love alone."

The End

APPENDIX

THE FOUR LAST THINGS

You have completed *The Final Destination,* a novel filled with fantasy and truth. Since my goal as an author of fiction is to invite readers to grow in faith, in this last section I present the formal teachings of the Catholic Church on death, eternal life, the particular judgment, Heaven, Purgatory, Hell and the Last Judgment.

I invite the readers to consider and meditate on the following paragraphs cited from the *Catechism of the Catholic Church.* The questions that follow may be used during personal prayer or for small group discussions.

Readers may access the *Catechism of the Catholic Church* by logging on to the Vatican website at:

http://www.vatican.va/archive/ENG0015/_INDEX.HTM .

ON EVERLASTING LIFE

1020 The Christian who unites his own death to that of Jesus views it as a step towards him and an entrance into everlasting life. When the Church for the last time speaks Christ's words of pardon and absolution over the dying Christian, seals him for the last time with a strengthening anointing, and gives him Christ in viaticum as nourishment for the journey, she speaks with gentle assurance:

Go forth, Christian soul, from this world in the name of God the almighty Father, who created you, in the name of Jesus Christ, the Son of the living God, who suffered for you, in the name of the Holy Spirit, who was poured out upon you. Go forth, faithful Christian!

May you live in peace this day, may your home be with God in Zion, with Mary, the virgin Mother of God, with Joseph, and all the angels and saints....

May you return to [your Creator] who formed you from the dust of the earth. May holy Mary, the angels, and all the saints come to meet you as you go forth from this life....

May you see your Redeemer face to face.

1. How does paragraph 1020 reveal the mercy of God at the hour of death?

2. What is the "final destiny" of the immortal soul?

THE PARTICULAR JUDGMENT

1021 Death puts an end to human life as the time open to either accepting or rejecting the divine grace manifested in Christ. The New Testament speaks of judgment primarily in its aspect of the final encounter with Christ in his second coming, but also repeatedly affirms that each will be rewarded immediately after death in accordance with his works and faith. The parable of the poor man Lazarus and the words of Christ on the cross to the good thief, as well as other New Testament texts speak of a final destiny of the soul—a destiny which can be different for some and for others.

1022 Each man receives his eternal retribution in his immortal soul at the very moment of his death, in a particular judgment that refers his life to Christ: either entrance into the blessedness of heaven-through purification or immediately, or immediate and everlasting damnation.

At the evening of life, we shall be judged on our love.

> *1. In Philippians 2:12, St. Paul urges us to work out our salvation in "fear and trembling." What does this mean and how does it apply in your life?*
>
> *2. In Luke 17:33, the evangelist quotes the Lord when he says "Whoever seeks to gain life will lose it, but whoever loses his life will preserve it." How do you explain this paradox?*

Words to know:

Trinity refers to the mystery of God in three Persons. We believe that God is Father, Son and Holy Spirit.

Saint refers to the "holy one" who leads a life in God's grace and receives the reward of Heaven after death.

HEAVEN

1023 Those who die in God's grace and friendship and are perfectly purified live forever with Christ. They are like God for ever, for they "see him as he is," face to face:

By virtue of our apostolic authority, we define the following: According to the general disposition of God, the souls of all the saints . . . and other faithful who died after receiving Christ's holy Baptism (provided they were not in need of purification when they died, . . . or, if they then did need or will need some purification, when they have been purified after death, . . .) already before they take up their bodies again and before the general judgment—and this since the Ascension of our Lord and Savior Jesus Christ into heaven - have been, are and will be in heaven, in the heavenly Kingdom and celestial paradise with Christ, joined to the company of the holy angels. Since the Passion and death of our Lord Jesus Christ, these souls have seen and do see the divine essence with an intuitive vision, and even face to face, without the mediation of any creature.

1024 This perfect life with the Most Holy Trinity—this communion of life and love with the Trinity, with the Virgin Mary, the angels and all the blessed—is called "heaven." Heaven is the ultimate end and fulfillment of the deepest human longings, the state of supreme, definitive happiness.

1025 To live in heaven is "to be with Christ." the elect live "in Christ," but they retain, or rather find, their true identity, their own names.

For life is to be with Christ; where Christ is, there is life, there is the kingdom.

1026 By his death and Resurrection, Jesus Christ has "opened" heaven to us. The life of the blessed consists in the full and perfect possession of the fruits of the redemption accomplished by Christ. He makes partners in his heavenly glorification those who have believed in him and remained faithful to his will. Heaven is the blessed community of all who are perfectly incorporated into Christ.

1027 This mystery of blessed communion with God and all who are in Christ is beyond all understanding and description.

Scripture speaks of it in images: life, light, peace, wedding feast, wine of the kingdom, the Father's house, the heavenly Jerusalem, paradise: "no eye has seen, nor ear heard, nor the heart of man conceived, what God has prepared for those who love him."

1028 Because of his transcendence, God cannot be seen as he is, unless he himself opens up his mystery to man's immediate contemplation and gives him the capacity for it. The Church calls this contemplation of God in his heavenly glory "the beatific vision":

How great will your glory and happiness be, to be allowed to see God, to be honored with sharing the joy of salvation and eternal light with Christ your Lord and God, . . . to delight in the joy of immortality in the Kingdom of heaven with the righteous and God's friends.

1029 In the glory of heaven the blessed continue joyfully to fulfill God's will in relation to other men and to all creation. Already they reign with Christ; with him "they shall reign for ever and ever."

1. In 1 Corinthians 2:9, St. Paul tells us about Heaven. He states: "no eye has seen, nor ear heard, nor the heart of man conceived, what God has prepared for those who love him." What does this reveal to you about eternal life?

2. What are our deepest longings that will be satisfied in Heaven? What are your deepest longings?

The Final Purification, or Purgatory

Word to know:

Purgatory comes from the Latin *purgare*, meaning to make clean or purify.

1030 All who die in God's grace and friendship, but still imperfectly purified, are indeed assured of their eternal salvation; but after death they undergo purification, so as to achieve the holiness necessary to enter the joy of heaven.

1031 The Church gives the name Purgatory to this final purification of the elect, which is entirely different from the punishment of the damned. The Church formulated her doctrine of faith on Purgatory especially at the Councils of Florence and Trent. The tradition of the Church, by reference to certain texts of Scripture, speaks of a cleansing fire:

As for certain lesser faults, we must believe that, before the Final Judgment, there is a purifying fire. He who is truth says that whoever utters blasphemy against the Holy Spirit will be pardoned neither in this age nor in the age to come. From this sentence we understand that certain offenses can be forgiven in this age, but certain others in the age to come.

1032 This teaching is also based on the practice of prayer for the dead, already mentioned in Sacred Scripture: "Therefore [Judas Maccabeus] made atonement for the dead, that they might be delivered from their sin." From the beginning the Church has honored the memory of the dead and offered prayers in suffrage for them, above all the Eucharistic sacrifice, so that, thus purified, they may attain the beatific vision of God. The Church also commends almsgiving, indulgences, and works of penance undertaken on behalf of the dead:

Let us help and commemorate them. If Job's sons were purified by their father's sacrifice, why would we doubt that our offerings for the dead bring them some consolation? Let us not hesitate to help those who have died and to offer our prayers for them.

1. Why is Purgatory a gracious gift from God?

2. How can we help the departed souls in Purgatory reach Heaven?

HELL

1033 We cannot be united with God unless we freely choose to love him. But we cannot love God if we sin gravely against him, against our neighbor or against ourselves: "He who does not love remains in death. Anyone who hates his brother is a murderer, and you know that no murderer has eternal life abiding in him." Our Lord warns us that we shall be separated from him if we fail to meet the serious needs of the poor and the little ones who are his brethren. To die in mortal sin without repenting and accepting God's merciful love means remaining separated from him forever by our own free choice. This state of definitive self-exclusion from communion with God and the blessed is called "hell."

1034 Jesus often speaks of "Gehenna" of "the unquenchable fire" reserved for those who to the end of their lives refuse to believe and be converted, where both soul and body can be lost. Jesus solemnly proclaims that he "will send his angels, and they will gather . . . all evil doers, and throw them into the furnace of fire," and that he will pronounce the condemnation: "Depart from me, you cursed, into the eternal fire!"

1035 The teaching of the Church affirms the existence of hell and its eternity. Immediately after death the souls of those who die in a state of mortal sin descend into hell, where they suffer the punishments of hell, "eternal fire." The chief punishment of hell is eternal separation from God, in whom alone man can possess the life and happiness for which he was created and for which he longs.

1036 The affirmations of Sacred Scripture and the teachings of the Church on the subject of hell are a call to the responsibility incumbent upon man to make use of his freedom in view of his eternal destiny. They are at the same time an urgent call to conversion: "Enter by the narrow gate; for the gate is wide and the way is easy, that leads to destruction, and those who enter by it are many. For the gate is narrow and the way is hard, that leads to life, and those who find it are few."

Since we know neither the day nor the hour, we should follow the advice of the Lord and watch constantly so that, when the single course of our earthly life is completed, we may merit to enter with him into the marriage feast and be numbered among the blessed, and not, like the wicked and slothful servants, be ordered to depart into the eternal fire, into the outer darkness where "men will weep and gnash their teeth."

1037 God predestines no one to go to hell; for this, a willful turning away from God (a mortal sin) is necessary, and persistence in it until the end. In the Eucharistic liturgy and in the daily prayers of her faithful, the Church implores the mercy of God, who does not want "any to perish, but all to come to repentance:"

Father, accept this offering from your whole family.

Grant us your peace in this life, save us from final damnation, and count us among those you have chosen.

1. If God our God is a God of love, how can Hell exist?

2. Why is Hell a choice?

THE LAST JUDGMENT

1038 The resurrection of all the dead, "of both the just and the unjust," will precede the Last Judgment. This will be "the hour when all who are in the tombs will hear [the Son of man's] voice and come forth, those who have done good, to the resurrection of life, and those who have done evil, to the resurrection of judgment." Then Christ will come "in his glory, and all the angels with him .... Before him will be gathered all the nations, and he will separate them one from another as a shepherd separates the sheep from the goats, and he will place the sheep at his right hand, but the goats at the left.... and they will go away into eternal punishment, but the righteous into eternal life."

1039 In the presence of Christ, who is Truth itself, the truth of each man's relationship with God will be laid bare. The Last Judgment will reveal even to its furthest consequences the good each person has done or failed to do during his earthly life: All that the wicked do is recorded, and they do not know. When "our God comes, he does not keep silence.". . . he will turn towards those at his left hand: . . . "I placed my poor little ones on earth for you. I as their head was seated in heaven at the right hand of my Father - but on earth my members were suffering, my members on earth were in need. If you gave anything to my members, what you gave would reach their Head. Would that you had known that my little ones were in need when I placed them on earth for you and appointed them your stewards to bring your good works into my treasury. But you have placed nothing in their hands; therefore you have found nothing in my presence."

1040 The Last Judgment will come when Christ returns in glory. Only the Father knows the day and the hour; only he determines the moment of its coming. Then through his Son Jesus Christ he will pronounce the final word on all history. We shall know the ultimate meaning of the whole work of creation and of the entire economy of salvation and understand the marvelous ways by which his Providence led everything towards its final end. The Last Judgment will reveal that God's justice triumphs over all the injustices committed by his creatures and that God's love is stronger than death.

1041 The message of the Last Judgment calls men to conversion while God is still giving them "the acceptable time, . . the day of salvation." It inspires a holy fear of God and commits them to the justice of the Kingdom of God. It proclaims the "blessed hope" of the Lord's return, when he will come "to be glorified in his saints, and to be marveled at in all who have believed."

> *1. Imagine the Last Day, at the end of the world, when the Lord will come to judge the living and the dead. Imagine that day will occur tomorrow at dawn. What might your prayers sound like tonight? What immediate changes would you make in your life?*

Made in the USA
Charleston, SC
02 February 2014